Rounders

A Novel by Kevin Canty

Based on the Screenplay by
D. J. Levien and Brian Koppelman

faber and faber

First published in 1998
by Faber and Faber Limited
3 Queen Square London WC1N 3AU

Published by arrangement with Hyperion,
114 Fifth Avenue, New York, New York 10011
Printed in England by
Mackays of Chatham PLC, Chatham, Kent

A CIP record for this book
is available from the British Library

ISBN 0–571–20036–2

2 4 6 8 10 9 7 5 3 1

rounders

ten-thirty at night and I'm standing outside Teddy KGB's place with thirty thousand dollars in my pocket, paralyzed. It's now or never, as Tony Bennett said. It's monkey time. I can't seem to move, is all.

Thirty thousand dollars is one hundred percent of the money I've got in the world. And Teddy's place is not in the best part of the city and that city is New York. Some asshole is going to come along and stick a gun in my face, I think, and I am going to deserve it because I am acting like an asshole myself. I have made up my mind to go into Teddy's and this is what I'm doing. What I am going to do. But I can't move forward and I can't move back and I just stand there on the sidewalk and I can see that I don't have the nerve for what I am about to do. I am going to deserve what happens to me. I'm shaking like a June bride and there is some cold and slushy thing like liquid nitrogen sloshing around in my colon and I think: Fuck me.

Stage fright, is all. It doesn't help to know it. I look around inside myself for the feeling I need and it isn't there—you know the feeling, eight feet tall and bulletproof, the place where even your fuckups turn out to be correct. I've got thirty thousand dollars, I tell myself, all mine. This starts me on the right track, knowing I've got the money. I can feel it in my pants pocket, a good-size bulge. It isn't just paper. I can feel the heat radiating off it. This starts to feel okay.

That, and knowing I'm cheating—not cheating straight up, it'd be worth your fucking life in Teddy's place, but cheating like stepping out on somebody. In this case, Jo. She doesn't know where I am or what I'm doing and she wouldn't like it if she did. Just a girlfriend, she doesn't have any special rights in the matter. Still, she wouldn't like it. This is another part of the feeling, the selfishness of it. I-me-mine. If she wants me, she can have me the way I am, and fuck the way she wants me to be. I know I'm trespassing. I don't care. I whisper to myself: This is my night, baby, mine all mine.

Fuck you. Here I come.

I say it under my breath, talking to nobody, the sidewalks, the city at large.

Then into the elevator (a rusty, creaky prison cell) and up and off at Teddy's floor. His place is a blank metal door. Whenever I knock I expect not to be answered, that they will all have picked up and gone, back to Russia, wherever. But this time he answers. The eye slot slides back and I can see that it is Teddy KGB himself giving me the eye, chewing on an Oreo cookie. He looks like he doesn't know me and then, slowly, he slides the eye slot back and the door opens for me.

The first thing that hits you is the smell, sweat and cigarette smoke, generations of sweat. That polyester they first made, the *Saturday Night Fever* stuff, it just doesn't wear out, and the fucking Russians love it. They wear that shit into the ground. You can't get the smell out of it. They loom in the dark outskirts of the room, the Russians do, around the little islands of light and green felt where the players are working. Something about that green, like the infield green, the promise of it. All mine, I remind myself. I-me-mine.

Teddy himself looks like a diseased bear, too skinny for his build and shedding. He's never seen daylight. He offers me an Oreo which I decline, then slides behind his desk—another small island of light—and starts to count out red and green checks.

"Five hundred?" he asks me.

"Not tonight, Teddy."

"No," he says. "What?"

"Three stacks of high society."

I pull the bills out as casually as I can, six paperclipped stacks of five thousand apiece, and hold them together in my hand. I watch Teddy's eyes: nothing. He sticks another Oreo in his mouth and chews it, slowly.

Then he seems to come to some kind of a decision. Without looking, without seeming to measure, he pushes a pile of gold and black checks toward me.

"Thirty thousand," he says. "Count it."

I take my money and I toss it on the desk, trying to be cool about it. I can't tell if I succeed, exactly. A little doubt surfaces again but it's gone right away—it's too late, showtime. Stage fright doesn't matter now. I count out the checks by the height of the stack and put them back in the rack: thirty thousand exactly. This is it, I think. I feel that liquid nitrogen running down my spine again, pitiful weakness but it's too late. Right or wrong.

The thing is, you play for a living, it's like any other job: you don't gamble, you grind it out. You win your one big bet an hour. Get your money in when you got the best of it, protect it when you don't, don't give anything away. Which I have been doing for one year, seven months, and thirteen days. I have built a bankroll, bet by bet. I have put myself through the first three semesters of law school. I have started to build myself a future, day by day and dollar by dollar. The big idea, though, that came to me—the bad idea, the idea that got me here—is this: if you're too careful, your life can become a fucking grind.

"It's right," I tell him.

"So, you're sitting the apple," he says. "Good. Want a cookie?"

"No."

He shrugs: nothing more to say. I'm just getting ready to get up and take my place when the exact wrong person comes out of the can, the guy I least wish to see in the whole fucking world: Joey Knish.

Immediately I get that caught feeling, busted. I know what he's going to say before he even knows I'm in the room. Joey's been a rounder, making his living at cards, since he was fifteen years old. If there's a degenerate on the scene in New York the last twenty years, Joey's either sat with him, bet with him, taken him, or been taken by him. He's a friend, right, but that doesn't mean I want to see him. If you're going to fuck up—and I don't know yet if I am or not—but if you're going to fuck up, it's better to do it in front of strangers. You don't want your friends around.

Immediately, like a psychic, he beelines for me and Teddy, eyeballing the rack of checks in front of me and then right at my face. He's pissed.

He says, "What're you, holding these for somebody?"

"Yeah," I tell him. "I'm holding 'em for you."

"You should be. I hope you're not thinking of putting all that glimmer into play."

I shrug and Joey looks around, like he's afraid of somebody catching us. Out of the corner of my eye, I can see Teddy's face: a little self-satisfied, cat that ate the canary. Which is exactly where I want him.

I don't want to go with Joey but I can't stop him, back into the darkest corner of the place. Here's another thing: when I get up to go with him, a quick annoyance crosses Teddy's face, like he's afraid of losing me. Just the way I want him.

"You don't want to butt onions with these guys," Joey says. "They'll chew you up. Take your whole bankroll."

"Thanks, Dad."

"What's that for?"

"You treat me like a fucking teenager, Joey."

"You act like a teenager, Mike. Thirty years old and you act like a fucking kid." For a second he's really mad and he lets me see it; then his guard goes back up again.

"Look," he says. "Plenty easy games. We get outta here, get some coffee, ride over to that soft seat in Queens."

"I'm sitting with the top guys tonight."

"You're not ready."

"Fuck you."

He looks hurt for a second but I've got a right. It doesn't stop him, anyway.

He says, "What I'm telling you is, I'm not the one who's going to get fucked, you sit no-limit with Teddy. Watch him from two tables away, fine. Stand on the rail, great. But don't sit down with him, you can only lose."

I don't say anything, though he expects me to. Joey can't seem to leave it alone.

"Why are you doing this?" he asks.

I'm starting to get pissed now. I don't need him to fuck with my luck or fuck with my confidence.

Joey says, "KGB didn't get that house up in Pound Ridge losing to part-time players like you."

"I know what I'm doing."

Joey looks at me, surprised. It's like I changed skin on him, turned into some different kind of animal.

"You're making a run at it, aren't you?" he says, dreamy, like he's thinking out loud. The ideas are coming at the same time as the words. "You're rolling up a stake and going to Vegas. I'm right, right?"

"I can beat the game."

"Maybe," Joey says. "Maybe this is a game can be beat. But you *know* you can beat the ten-twenty at the Chesterfield, and the Hi-Lo at that goulash joint on Seventy-ninth Street."

He gives me the big sad eye, like a golden retriever or something, and I know I'm disappointing him, and I know—I *know*—that from everything that's happened to him in his life, that he's right and I'm wrong. I just got a little different feeling is all. He stares at me for thirty seconds longer, pleading, then all of a sudden gives up.

"Okay, Mike," he says. "I understand, I understand . . . back to battle, then."

A final sigh; then, like sleepwalkers, each of us drifts off to take the role we've been assigned for the evening. Joey Knish rejoins a table of regulars, red, green, and white checks on the table in front of them—the table where I ought to be, where I would be any night

6

but this—while I go back over to Teddy's desk and collect my gold and black, my specials.

KGB leaves the front desk in the care of one of his Russians and tails me into the back room, big fish little fish. I don't know how many of these Russians he's got or where he gets them, but there always seems to be another. Even the meat hanging around the rail, you can't tell who's working for Teddy. All of them maybe. This is Indian country.

The crowd parts for Teddy, not for me.

The game is Texas Hold 'Em, no-limit, twenty-five-thousand-dollar minimum buy-in. There are already eight players at the table when we get there and nasty-looking they are: bad haircuts, worse rugs, skin the color of wet cement and bags and sags of flesh under everything. Some of them I recognize. The only half-assed respectable-looking one is Irving, which is because he's Hasidic. The rest of them dress like they were the last to get to the garage sale. The only thing you notice, the only thing that sets them off, is that every one of them is wearing a ring, and I mean a fucking rock. These guys are pros, every one. They've sat at this table before, and they can afford to sit here now.

"You know Mike," Teddy says, hand on my back like he's sponsoring me.

And the players look up and nod and a couple of them smile but it looks like it hurts them to do it. A shuffle and scrape of chairs and then I'm at the table, Teddy sitting opposite. No-limit games don't come together often outside the casinos. The stakes attract rich flounders, and they in turn attract the sharks. Pros from three states at least are sitting around this table, talking about nothing, fidgeting with their checks, eyeing me sideways to see which one I am, flounder or shark. Nobody knows yet.

This guy I know, Sy, is opening a fresh deck. He looks like a monk, with his little fringe of hair around the outside, but he isn't. Everybody watches, pretending not to. I stick a cigarette in the corner of my mouth—I don't light it, it's just there to keep my fucking mouth shut—and then Sy deals out the hand and we are off and running.

Texas Hold 'Em is the Cadillac of poker, what the big boys play exclusively: two cards down to every player, then five more across the middle of the table, community cards that everyone can use to make a hand. The first three come together, all at once, which is called the flop. The next one is called the turn and the last one is the river.

"Blinds up," says a guy I don't recognize, and the first two guys to Sy's left put in their checks. I take a peek at my hole cards—a jack and a seven, nothing—but the bet stays cheap and I stay in for the flop and I'm already trying to read the table, who's got what. This is just for practice. I'm not going anywhere with these cards. But this is not a game of cards at all. There's cards in it, sure, and maybe a little luck, but what I'm playing is the nine other faces at the table and not the fifty-two pieces of cardboard. If I don't know what you've got, then I'm betting blind, and betting blind, like driving blind, is not such a good idea.

After the flop, the bet goes around to Irving, the Hasidic guy. He pushes eight black chips into the pot.

"Raise," he says. "An eight ball."

That's enough for me. I toss my hand into the muck.

"South Street," I say.

"Ouch," says the guy next to me, and tosses his cards, and so does Teddy KGB.

By the time we make it to the river there's just three in, Irving, Kenny, and Savino. Kenny I know from around, a little, ex-jock the size of a fucking house. You couldn't pry his face open with a crowbar. Savino I know by reputation, which is mixed: Italian guy, sharp dresser circa 1965, with one of those haircuts you see in the windows of old barber shops, straight back and pouffed out and sprayed.

Around it goes, just once, and Kenny pushes the last bet in.

"Call, Irv," he says, turning a pair of aces. "Take a suck on these babies—the Brass Brazilians."

Irving flips a pair of queen.

"Fucking spikes crush my ladies," he says, and flips them into the muck. Savino folds without a word.

Irving gets up from the table, ready to take a break, but Kenny is just starting to enjoy himself. "You know," he says, "truth be told, Irving, I'm surprised to see a guy like you in here in the first place."

"That's the thing with the skullcaps," Savino says. "The big con. Everyone thinks they're beyond reproach, but some of the biggest fucking degenerates I know wear them."

"Don't talk that way about my people," Irving says.

"Your people," Savino snorts. "Please, Irv, you're the only Jew I know who took Germany plus the points."

Hard to say if this gets home or not; Irving isn't showing either way. He waves Savino off and leaves. The chatter and fidgeting settle back into the always groove: cigarettes lit and flicked and stubbed out and fumbled for, backs and necks scratched, clothing adjusted. I set my baseball cap on my head again, myself. Kenny collects his checks in front of him and Sy collects the cards for a fresh deal and, in the process, takes a few of Kenny's checks with him.

I see it, and I can't be the only one.

He could make it right, he's got all the second chances he needs. Nobody's going to hold it against him.

Then innocently, casually, bored as hell, he stacks the checks out of the pot with his own. The old professor.

"Fucking cocksucker," Savino breathes out, automatically. Then says it again, out loud: "Teddy, this fucking cocksucker—what's your name, Sy?—just fucking kited the pot."

The talk just falls off the table, players and spectators. It seems like there's one line of light and Sy's in the exact dead center of it.

"Who?" he says.

There's a general movement where everybody inches closer to their stacks, ready to cover the checks if this blows up.

"You," Savino says. "I saw you rake the chips in and put them in your stack."

"No, no," Sy says. "Those? A few, by accident. I was about to give them to Kenny."

"I waited to see," Savino says. "Once you stacked them, you stole them."

Now everybody starts talking, everybody's got their two cents' worth. I'm with them. Then Sy turns to me and he's pleading with his eyes, pleading for a break.

"You know me," Sy says to me. "You've seen me around, I wouldn't . . ."

But this is enough. I can feel the eyes of the others on the two of us and I'm not going to be dragged into the spotlight with him.

"I don't know this guy," I say. "I'm not with him."

Finally Teddy KGB speaks up.

"Get out of here," he says to Sy.

The old man opens his mouth to explain but Teddy cuts him off.

"No," Teddy says. "I saw it."

Sy arranges his face into a picture of innocence, a poor man trampled by injustice, and starts to collect his checks.

"Leave it," Teddy says.

"What?"

"I said fucking go," Teddy says. He flicks his eyes, somewhere in the darkness beyond the table, and three of the Russians materialize around Sy. He looks at me one more time, he tries to plead. I don't even look away, I just go blank. The Russians move him along and toward the door and out and Sy doesn't even try to run, not even when the first one spins him around and the first fist lands in his gut. They're starting to kick already when the door eases shut behind them and still, Sy doesn't make a sound. Impressive performance for a dumb fuck, I think. All the soft places in New York this guy could have picked for check copping, and he had to try Teddy KGB's. For a few hundred a hand, he loses his whole buy-in. Not to mention a few years off his life.

"Fucking cocksucker," Savino says again. "You believe this fucking guy, coming in here?"

Teddy counts out the stolen checks, back to Kenny, then hands the rest of Sy's stack to one of his Russians. Another takes away the empty chair. Sy never existed.

"Okay," Teddy KGB says. "Let's play some cards."

The rattle and snap of a deck being shuffled calls us back to attention. The chairs shift back into place—eight now, with Irving and Sy gone—and then the hole cards come out, and the game starts again, and there isn't time or thought enough to worry about anything but the game: who's got what, who's working on what, the ten thousand possibilities and everybody's little secret in the hole. A hand or two in, I remember that I know how to do this. I belong here. Looking around the table, it's not a club that anybody would brag about joining—these guys are the ones who eat at the restaurants where you wonder if anybody ever eats there, they twitch and shuffle and insult each other. Your daughter comes home on prom night with any of these guys, she's going to miss the prom.

But this is where I belong, right here. Under the big light. There isn't time for anything but this: a game that's big as big time gets, the best players, the biggest money, the best chance of things going haywire plus or minus. No limit. There's no other game in which fortunes can change so much from hand to hand. A brilliant player can get a strong hand cracked, go on tilt, and lose his mind along with every single chip in front of him. This is why the World Series of Poker is decided over a No-limit Hold 'Em table.

Some people, pros even, won't play no-limit. They can't handle the swings. Some people think it's the only pure game left. Doyle Brunson says this, and he's the man who wrote The Book, the Bible, *The Super System.* I guess I feel the same way. Like Papa Wallenda said: "Life is on the wire. The rest is just waiting."

No waiting tonight. It's all I can do just to keep track of the possibilities. I'm playing all right, I can feel it. I'm playing with discipline, folding the hands where I've got nothing in the hole, but I'm not afraid to bet, either. I catch Savino trying to steal a pot, take him down with three kings, which feels all right. A confidence-builder. All the time, though, I can feel Teddy KGB across the table from me, watching, waiting. I know it's going to come down to me and him at some point. I watch him unscrew another Oreo and put it in his mouth, some hand we're both out of the late betting, and he catches me watching him and he grins at me. His teeth are black with cookie mush and some other horrible color underneath. I think that the last fucking place in the world you'd want to be is the inside of Teddy's mouth.

I don't want to focus too much on him though. I don't want to lose track of the other guys. Savino, for instance: maybe he looks like he's listened to one too many Frankie Valli records, maybe he acts like a schmuck from New Jersey, but underneath that haircut is a mind like a good watch, ticking away. He doesn't miss many percentages. He's smart, is his way of getting through it. Kenny isn't quite as smart, from what I can see, but he's got a talent for the bluff. He plays by the numbers just fine and then once in a while he goes off the deep end and you'll never know which is which. Then there's this guy Henry Lin, who comes in later— Asian guy, forty or so, wire-rimmed glasses and a baseball cap. He used to be a college professor, used to design computers, that's the legend on him. Everybody's got something here. Everybody's got an edge. Everybody but me. The saying goes like this: If you can't spot the sucker in your first half hour at the table, then *you* are the sucker.

And I haven't spotted the sucker yet.

A little chill again but this is different. This isn't the fear. This is what I came for: the high wire.

Time passes. I don't know where it goes, I don't stop to think or recognize the passing. There's just the cards, the faces, the checks flowing back and forth across the table. The players come and go—Irving drops back in for a while, some idiot in a cowboy hat who doesn't last an hour—and then more of them go and I think it's getting late. I can't even tell. It doesn't matter until you need food or you can't think anymore and I'm nowhere close to gone. Come on, I think. Bring it on. It could be three in the afternoon or three in the morning and none of this would change: the lights, the smoke, the sour nervous smell or the electrical feel of money changing hands, luck appearing and disappearing.

Finally it's down to four of us: Henry Lin, Savino, me, and Teddy KGB. I'm doing fine. The thirty thousand I started with has turned to fifty—not off these guys, most of it, but off the ones who left. The fish in the cowboy hat was extra good to me. Here's a hint: If you can't keep that little smile out of the corner of your mouth when you're looking at a good hand, don't try to bluff. Either that or stay out of the expensive games. Our cowboy friend, he spent a lot of money on this lesson and then he left and he still didn't know.

I'm dealing, anyway. The blind bets go in. I've got a good feeling, not that I'm letting myself get undisciplined but what I know is working. I can stay with these guys. I take a peek at my hole cards: ace of clubs and nine of clubs, not great but workable.

Lin dumps his cards and says, "Fold."

"I gotta raise," I say. "Five hundred."

Teddy looks at me. "That's a position raise," he finally says. "I call it."

"Pasadena," Savino says, and folds his hand.

Me and Teddy, all that's left. Just then Joey Knish comes into the room, into my line of sight, and all my wishing in the world won't make him go away. He's distracting me, psyching me. I don't want him watching.

The flop, anyway: the eight of clubs, nine of spades, ace of spades. Two pair and counting. This one is mine, I can feel it. And here's the beauty of this game: I flop top two, and I want to keep him in the hand. Against your average guy I'd set a bear-trap—hardly bet at all—let him walk into it. But KGB's too smart for that. So what I've got to do is overbet the pot—make it look like I'm trying to buy it. Then he plays back at me, and I get paid off.

That's the plan, anyway.

"Two thousand," I tell him. "The bet's two thousand dollars."

He looks at me. He takes another of those fucking cookies and slowly chews on it for a minute and only then does he decide.

"I call," he says, pushing his own stack of checks toward the middle. "Burn and turn."

Nine of hearts.

I try to keep it off my face: full house, nines full of aces. I put Teddy on a flush draw.

"To the bettor," Teddy says.

"Check's good," I say, trying to keep him in the hand. Now I'm praying for a spade to fall so Teddy can make his flush. He makes his hand, he'll bet it strong. I've watched him. Come on, I think, come on.

The river card: queen of spades.

Las Vegas, I think: next stop, the fucking Mirage. I've got him cold, cold, cold if I can keep it off my fucking face.

"I'm going to bet," Teddy says. "Bet, fifteen thousand."

He pushes a stack of checks into the pot, he pushes in a new car I'm going to be driving next week.

"Time," I tell him, and I make it look like I'm wondering whether to stay in. I try to look worried. Really, I'm counting my money, making my reservations for Vegas. I pretend to think for a few seconds.

"I don't think you've got spades," I tell him, trying to make it sound uncertain as I can. "I'm going to raise, Teddy."

I count it out—everything I've fucking got—and push the checks into the table, bare-naked felt in front of me.

"All in," I tell him. "Thirty-three thousand."

"You're right," he says, shoving stacks of chips after mine. "I don't have spades."

But he doesn't even need to say it, I can see it in his body, the speed he shoves the chips in with, the little hoggish way he licks his lips: I have fucked the dog.

He flips the pair of aces upward on the table.

"Aces full, Mike."

He smiles at me—he *smiles* at me—then rakes the pot in quickly. Lin and Savino drop away somewhere. They don't want to look at me. The game is over. Teddy had me all along. He knew, all the way through. Every nickel I had. Every fucking nickel. One of the Russians shows up with a couple of racks and Teddy stacks the checks back in them and then he is gone, too.

This is all my doing.

Nobody wants to stand anywhere near me. Then Knish comes up behind me and pats me on the shoulder and in that minute I'm more pissed at him than anyone: for being right. He was my friend and he told me I didn't have it in me and he was right.

"C'mon, get up," he says. "Walk it off."

"I can't move."

"We'll talk about it. I'll buy you breakfast. Then we can go over to the Tenth Street Baths and have a schvitz."

"I couldn't even afford the steam."

"Come on," he says, and this time it's not a suggestion—it's an order. I get up, follow him toward the door. Wherever I pass, people stop talking and stare. A fifty-thousand-dollar swing is a rare deal. It's hard to find that big of a schmuck. I feel like I'm all by myself in the middle of a little circle of silence and bad luck and stupidity. I didn't have it and I thought I did.

Outside Joey lights a joint, offers it to me. I start to turn him down—I want to stay sharp—and then I remember there's nothing to stay sharp for. Not a fucking thing.

"Tapped," he says. "Didn't leave yourself any outs."

"I'm down to the felt, Knish. Lost my whole bankroll. My case money and my tuition, too."

He says, "Happens to everyone. Time to time everyone goes bust. You'll be back in the game before you know it."

I shake my head as soon as he says it. Suddenly I *know*.

"I'm done, Joey. I'm out of it."

"They all say that at first," he says. "Anyway, let me stake you. Standard deal, fifty percent of your winnings. You lose, it's on me."

That little spark of hope flies up when he says it and then I remember: I haven't got it.

"I'd just throw it away," I tell him. "You still got your truck?"

"I've got the truck," he says. "Are you ready for the truck? You sure?"

"I'm sure," I tell him. "Bring it on."

ne last little errand: I've got to tell Jo.

I get home, seven in the morning, which she is used to. Sometimes we cross paths, her already making coffee in her bathrobe while I come in stinking of cigarette smoke and sweat, the last unshaven mess of the night meeting up with the first sticky mess of the morning.

Other times, though, it's like we meet somewhere in between. She's a little bit of a night owl herself, a day sleeper, and she doesn't mind being woken up. It's a nice moment: four or five or even six in the morning, the first little birdies of daylight already going off and us in the bedroom talking. She sleeps naked, which is a plus. Sometimes she'll have a drink, she'll make me bring her a glass of wine and I'll have a beer and we'll talk about things, end-of-the-night things: a joke somebody told, a hot streak or a cold one. Nights I would bring home a thousand dollars or two and spread it across the bed like confetti. Jo didn't mind. She likes the action, if you ask me—a Connecticut girl, with the cheekbones and the hair. Where she was brought up, nothing ever happened.

Tonight though. This may be a little more action than she wants.

I let myself into the apartment quietly, wondering if I want to do this now or sleep it off, tell her tomorrow. First light of morning. It's weird, something happens and you feel like a burglar in your own fucking apartment. It's more hers than mine by now though—her rugs, her sofas, her chairs and dishes. I was pretty much camping out in here when we met. It's better now. But I don't know, you know, the way the furniture and shit seemed to be looking at me like I was guilty. She goes for the modern stuff, you know, the furniture from Sweden. All these clean reasonable lines.

What it is, it's all daylight stuff.

It's one of the things I've figured out, the difference between nighttime and day. In the daylight, I want different things than in the night. In the daylight, I want to be clean and reasonable and respectable. I want the kind of practical life these chairs seem to have. So I come in at four in the morning with a thousand dollars of dirty money in my pocket—literally dirty, soft with handling, faded—and the fucking furniture wants to talk to me about it.

In the daylight, I don't want to get drunk. I don't want to sleep with anybody but Jo. In the daylight, I have no desire to run a busted flush right past the table with my head held high and come home with a wad of cash. I want the things that are good for me and I don't want the scheme or the scam or the hustle, the pure joy of getting away with it, I-me-mine . . . okay, I think: You win. The furniture wins. I will be good and responsible and I will live in the daytime and eat my shit like everybody else.

Jo is sleeping when I come in but she wakes up halfway when I turn on the light.

"Time is it?" she asks.

"Bedtime," I tell her. "You go back to sleep."

She shakes it off though, her eyes slowly clearing as I take my shoes and socks off, my shirt. She sits up, wearing the sheet wrapped around her like a toga party, her eyes slowly clearing into the dim light. I'm in shorts and an undershirt, sitting on the edge of the bed, looking out the window, which is closed by the blinds—anyplace away from her eyes.

"So, how'd you do tonight?" she asks.

"Can we skip it?"

"What's the matter?"

I just shrug.

"Bad night," I tell her.

"How bad?"

"You want a drink?"

She actually considers this for a moment. "No," she says, "I've got a meeting at ten."

"I'm busted, Jo. I'm on the truck."

"What does that mean?"

"It means the usual. The money is gone."

"All of it?"

"All of it."

This takes a minute to register. But when it does, it's like I slapped her: the color comes up in her cheeks and her eyes are all lit up. She's pissed, no doubt.

"Christ, Mike, that was thirty thousand dollars. That was a house in Nebraska or something."

"If you want to live in Nebraska."

But no joke of mine is going to slow her down.

"Thirty thousand dollars," she says. "You spent it in a *night*. How in the hell did you do that?"

"Playing over at Teddy's."

"Playing what?"

"No-limit," I say—and I can barely squeeze the words out, I'm that embarrassed for myself. My lips are curling, acting weird.

"No-limit," she says. "No-limit with Teddy KGB. That's pretty wonderful, Mike. That's pretty smart. Jesus, Mike, you told me yourself."

"I know," I tell her. "I know. You want a drink now?"

"Yep," she says. "Yes, I do."

I get her a glass of white wine. When I come back, she's sitting up a little straighter in bed with the sheet wrapped a little tighter around her, a little higher up on her chest. This is not the way she looks when she's feeling generous and forgiving. She takes the glass without thanks and sips. Sometime when I was out of the room, she raised the blinds on the window and turned out the light, and now the first gray light is in the room. She's keeping her eyes from me, watching the rooftops across the alley.

"You're on the truck," she says. "What does that mean, anyway? I've heard you say it before."

"I told you this before," I say, but she shakes her head no. "It's Joey's truck, Joey Knish. He bought it a few years ago, started running a route where you deliver beverages and baked goods and stuff like that, to the Bronx all the way up into Westchester. That's why they call him Joey Knish. I told you all that."

"Maybe," she says. She isn't giving me a fucking thing this morning.

"It's what you do when you're tapped out," I tell her. "Joey got off it when the cards warmed up for him but he held onto the route. There's always somebody to take it."

"Now it's your turn," Jo says.

"Now it's my turn."

There's a moment of silence, where I think anything could happen: she'll slap me, she'll kiss me, she'll get up and walk out. She's next to me and naked but I might as well be on Mars for all the attention she's paying. Still I know she's thinking about me. She's wondering about me, who I am.

"Thirty thousand dollars in one night," she finally says. "That's not bad. I mean, that's a *big* mistake, isn't it, Mikey?"

"It wasn't a mistake."

This wakes her up again. She looks at my face, sharply.

"What do you mean, not a mistake?"

"All in," I tell her, and suddenly I want her to understand. "That's the only way to play it, all in. Nothing held back. I wanted to see how good I was. I mean, I could half-ass along for years, playing along with Knish, all the other guys, and I'd never know if I could really play, you know, if I could keep up with the best. Now I know."

"Yeah, but Jesus, Mike—the money."

"That's where the money came from," I tell her. "It's just a way of keeping score."

"Not out here," she says. "Not in the real world."

"I tell you what—right before the end I was up fifty, Jo, sitting with the big boys with fifty thousand dollars on the table in front of me and for that moment I was fucking golden. Untouchable. I've never had that feeling before but I've been looking for it all my life. What's that car your father drives?"

"It's a Lexus."

"That car cost fifty thousand dollars, easy. You think he gets a feeling like that every time he sits his ass down on the leather? I don't think so, Jo. I mean, I was *golden*."

"For a little while."

"For about half an hour."

"That's an expensive ride," she says. "I mean, I'm sorry, Mike—I know you feel lousy enough without me piling on. I just can't let go of the money, I guess. The waste of it."

"What money?" I ask her. "The thirty thousand I left the house with? The twenty I picked up in the game? The five hundred I started with two years ago? I mean, I wish I'd held onto my tuition money."

"You spent your tuition money?"

"I didn't *spend* it," I tell her. "I *bet* it. There's a difference."

"I guess I don't see the difference. You had it. Now you don't have it."

All of a sudden I get impatient. It's just words we're making out of this, and the words won't tell the feeling. Jo doesn't understand and she isn't going to understand and it really doesn't matter.

"Look," I tell her. "It doesn't matter."

"What do you mean?"

"I'm done," I tell her.

"Done with what?"

"The whole thing. I quit."

The silence rises up between us again, the one where she's wondering about me. This is exactly what I would say if I was lying, which she knows. Except this time I'm not lying.

"Look," I tell her, eye-to-eye. "That was the whole point of this. I just wanted to go all-out, all-in, everything on the table. I just wanted to give it a shot, see if I could keep up. Which I almost could. So now I know."

"You're not going to just quit."

"I already did," I tell her. "The minute I walked out of there."

"I don't believe you," she says, and for the first time this morning she seems interested in me. I can suddenly smell her body, her perfume, which wasn't there before—that mystery thing that women have, the way they can turn it off and on. I'm *her* nighttime thing, I can see that. It's when I'm lying, when I'm cheating, when I'm rolling around in bed with her and a thousand dollars of somebody else's money that I become interesting to her. I don't know what inside her wants this but something does—maybe the thing that was bored shitless in high school in Connecticut, maybe the 3.94 average undergrad at Brown. She's a smart girl, Jo. She's going to marry a suit and have a nice life.

"Maybe it's time anyway," she says.

"About time."

"It's a hell of a way to find out though. What are you going to do for money?"

"Like I said, I'm on the truck. Midnight to whenever, starting tomorrow."

"I don't know," she says. "I don't know if poor but honest suits you. The Horatio Alger boy."

"I don't know either," I tell her. But by then she's got her hand around the back of my neck, she's cradling my head, and as soon as she does I can feel how tired I am. She pulls me toward her. I let my head drop onto her chest and the sheet slips a little and she's still naked under there. Not that anything is going to happen this morning. It's too late, or too early. Just this moment of rest, you know? Where the spinning stops, and everything slows down to where you can touch it, where you can feel it. I want to stay there and for a minute, while I'm sliding off into sleep, it feels like I can.

the truck, though: the truck is a bitch, a beatup GMC C60 ten-ton truck that's been spraypaint-tagged and painted over white and tagged again. The inside of the cab smells like cigarette smoke and spilled coffee and somebody tossed their lunch in there once, a long time ago. The brakes are sketchy. The dashboard light for the gas gauge doesn't work, so Joey keeps a Bic lighter up on the speedometer, which I use to see if I'm out yet. It's the kind of truck where people automatically give you the finger when they see you, whether you're doing anything wrong or not.

The route is worse: every beat-up off-brand all-night convenience store between Yankee Stadium and Westchester. Worse: Knish told somebody who told somebody that I was in law school, so now every one of these clerks has got me down. It's two, three, four in the morning. These clerks have got nothing to do but worry about getting robbed, all night long, sitting there with a target on the front of their shirt. So it's like, Test Your Legal Knowledge time when Mikey comes with the Little Debbies and the Ding-Dongs.

"Lemme ask you something," Moogie says. Moogie is maybe forty-three, three hundred pounds easy, lives with his mom—he told me! He's got his red polyester Sip'N'Go vest on, which fits him like a pup tent. He chews Copenhagen on the sly and spits into an empty Coke can, thinking nobody will notice.

"In a legal sense," he says, "can Steinbrenner really move the Yankees? Does he have the fucking right to just move them?"

"How do I know?" I ask him.

"You didn't learn that yet?"

"No," I tell him. "I think they teach about Steinbrenner the third year of law school."

"I was wondering that."

"What?"

"You know, how many years of law school there were. Like, are you a lawyer right now?"

"Not yet, Moogie."

"I guess it's different with doctors," he says, squinting down to try to decode the order slip, finally giving up. But before he signs he's got to talk.

"I had my mom down in the hospital," he says. "You know, with the emphysema and all. Did I tell you about that?"

"I remember," I tell him, a flat-out lie. But I would rather chew my leg out of a bear trap than listen to the story of his mother's disease. Every minute with Moogie is a minute I don't get to sleep.

"Anyway, they had this fucking zip take a look at her, you know, Q-Tip motherfucker. And it turns out he's not even a fucking doctor! He's what they call a resident. So that's what I was wondering."

"What?"

"Whether you were like a lawyer resident or what. You know?"

"Sign it, Moogie, please. There's no such thing."

"So there's no, like—"

"Three years of school, you take a test, then you're a lawyer. That's it."

"I was just wondering," he says. Then looks down again, holds the order slip up, looks over at the coolers and the rack of snack cakes. "This all straight?"

"Christ, Moogie, yeah I think so."

Still he doesn't want to let me go. Once I'm gone, he's back to all-alone again and waiting for the felons with the big handguns. This big fat pile of need. Not my fault.

"Sign it or I'll sign it myself," I tell him. "I'm behind."

"Fuck you. I got to make sure it's straight."

"It's straight. Look, Moogie, I short you on a case of Little Debbies, I don't get to be a lawyer anymore, okay? Two years of expensive education down the toilet. So please."

"I didn't know that," Moogie says, and finally takes up his ballpoint and signs. I leave him there alone. I drive off, alone, to the next and the next and the next, all night long.

This goes on through the rest of the fall, through the dead part of winter, and on into the first false spring and every morning I think it's going to end. This can't be living. I'm sleeping maybe five hours a night, and in my dreams I'm pushing a hand truck full of soda pop down a long, long hallway or driving the truck when the brakes do finally go. The thing with a bad job is that you can't get it off you. It's like some kind of grease or film, it sticks to you, you can't shower it off. And okay: I'm making enough off the route to keep the tuition up and make my half of the rent—Jo, like a lot of skinny girls, has got a little bit of bookkeeper in her—but every day I wake up and I think: Last day, today's the last day. Maybe I'm not cut out for this life. Maybe I like myself better as a cardplayer—even a second-rate cardplayer—than I do as a delivery boy.

But then I remind myself that I have a future, that I am making myself a future. That I'm going to have to fit in a suit if I want to stay with Jo. Plus I like the idea of myself in a good suit, making some money, going out. A lawyer—I don't know, it seems kind of halfway between the straight world and the hustle. All that I-me-mine. But sometimes I don't know if this is even my own fantasy that I'm after or whether it's just some dream I lifted from TV, from watching too many Michael Douglas movies.

And then I remind myself that it doesn't fucking matter what I think about all this, that I have to do it anyway. This is the life I have made for myself and I have to live it. This is the easiest thing to believe when the alarm goes off at ten in the morning after I made it in at five: just keep moving, don't fall down. Jo can smell that little sticky failure grease on me already. I do what I can and more. I don't want to spend the rest of my life trying to wash the smell of failure out of my hair.

So: I get up, I grind and grind and grind some more. Jo helps. We study together, just like in the fucking Archie comics, except that what we study is even more boring than high school.

Springtime comes to the law library in the form of moot court: real judges, real cases. First we face off against other teams from City Law; then, if we win, we get to go on against other law schools. It's good for me, I think—keeps me in the library, in the books—because I like to win. I want to win. They even made me captain of the fucking team.

"Two more weeks," Jo says. We're in the law library, ten o'clock on a spring night, ass-deep in paper while the world is having fun

28

outside. The only reason she's talking at all is that she's waiting for something to print out on her computer.

She says, like she's talking to herself, "We might make it, we might not."

"How do you expect me to concentrate?" I ask her.

She looks at me, almost surprised to find me there.

"What?" she says.

"On the work," I tell her. "How am I supposed to concentrate with you sitting next to me looking like that?"

She laughs. "What did you do, take a correspondence course in charm school when I wasn't looking? You still got to do the work, Michael."

"I'm very serious about the work," I tell her, using my best bright-young-man face. And I get her going on it, too. She does a slow double take and then sees that I'm faking her out and she gives me a sharp little flick with her fingernail on the skin of my arm.

"Yeah," she says, "that look might induce *me* to give you a passing grade. But I'm not the one scoring the exams. Now define 'taking under false pretenses.' "

"Listen, you just get me through the Mulligan, I'll worry about the rest."

"You know, if we win, we get to face off with Columbia. And they're a tough bunch."

"Tough?" I ask her. I think about Teddy KGB and his Russians, the way he could snap his fingers and suddenly there's a side of beef in a polyester shirt, ready to do you harm. Them versus Columbia. I'd pay to see it.

"Well, they're rich," I tell her, "and they've all been bred for this shit."

29

I take the last pages of her file out of the printer and collate them and hand them to her, more shit. Papers and papers and papers.

"That's it for this," I tell her. "Can we be done now?"

"Your commitment inspires me," she says; stretches, looks at her watch. "All right, let's go."

"I'll drop this stuff off with Petrovsky, you go on home. I've still got to hit my route."

"Again," she says. "Jesus, how long can you keep up this schedule? Don't you miss sleeping in the same bed as me?"

"Sleep's overrated."

"Who's talking about sleep?" she asks.

I quit packing my briefcase, slip around next to her, and hugging and kissing, and I can feel the empty place where I need her. Not just sex, though sex would suit me just fine. She's turned around to face me and I can feel her body through her clothes. Pressed against the table, her hips are solid up against mine and for a second, for one small second, I think it might happen: "Man Nails Girlfriend In Law Library."

Not this girlfriend though. She pushes me off, just when things are getting interesting, gives me one of her Significant Glances—somewhere between "I told you so" and "See what you're missing?"—and finishes packing her briefcase. And right here I'm feeling it again, where I don't see how I can go on living like this. It's got to end sometime, sometime soon.

Then we're out on the street, it's spring and warm and the trees are starting to come out in leaves. It's spring for everybody but us. I put Jo in a cab and let her go, her with her briefcase and me with mine. It's worth it, I tell myself. It isn't worth it. It's got to be worth it.

Petrovsky's office is in the old faculty building. I've never been in here at night before: dark deserted hallways, built in the fifties, like the headquarters of some company that went out of business a long time ago. I still have that feeling that I'm making a mistake, that I'm wasting my time, and these hallways are just reminding me. My own footsteps echo in my ears.

The office doors are dark, all but one: Petrovsky's. I can hear men's talk, smell cigar smoke, and so I knock and wait a moment before I go in.

Six faces look up at me when I come in, all men, all stern, all pissed-off at the interruption: all judges, except for Petrovsky, who is only dean of the law school. On the table between them are cards and chips, drinks and ashtrays. I have managed to walk in on the Judges' Game.

"Michael," Petrovsky says, waving me in the door. "You've got some things for me?"

The other's relax a little, but they still have me in their sights. The Judges' Game: I'd heard about it on the street, before I was even in law school. A rotating group of ten or twelve judges, prosecutors, and professors. They all have money, and in my playing days it would have been pretty sweet to have any of them owing me favors. Only problem is, no one can get into the game anymore. One rounder, Crispy Linetta, sat in under some pretense. But when they found out he was a pro, he couldn't cross the street without a legal hassle. Even his regular club, Vorshay's, got shut down. The place had been open since 1907.

Now the judges are judging me. It looks like they're used to it. A big cheese-faced man puts his cigar down and bores into me.

"Kid," he says. "He paying you for this late-night shit?"

"Knowledge is my only reward, sir."

"Let me tell you, it ain't worth it," the big guy says. "Why don't you become a jockey? Do something useful."

Kaplan—Judge Kaplan, Court of Appeals, one of the faces I do know—comes to my defense: "The kid's a little tall for a jockey, isn't he, Gene?"

Gene, I think—who the fuck is it? I ought to know who the big guy is.

"Enough with the Belmont recruiting spiel," says a tough guy, obvious cop or ex-cop. "The bet's to you, Kappy."

I came in halfway through a hand of seven-card stud, the hole cards and half of the face cards already dealt. Now that my novelty's worn off, the judges start to turn back toward their hands, rechecking their down cards to see if they remember them right.

But Petrovsky isn't done networking for me. He says to the big guy, Gene: "Michael is heading the defense in the moot court you're presiding over next week. Besides, he needs the background if he's going to clerk for one of you this summer."

Oh, shit, I think: Our pal Gene is Judge Eugene Marinacci of the New York Supreme Court. I quickly go back over everything I might have said to see if I've ended my career yet.

"Abe, I thought you liked the kid," says one of the others, a face I can't place. "Why do you want to make him a civil servant?"

The cop-looking guy leans over to me and winks. "Word to the wise," he says. "Stay in the private sector. That Nassau defense attorney's game—they use our chips for coasters."

This guy would be the D.A., I think—Shields is his name. This is my future, right here, assuming I'm going to have one. The card game gradually starts up again, the center of attention again. I settle in next to Petrovsky as my friend and protector in this bunch, though as dean of the fucking school, he's usually a pretty intimidating figure. He is the least-important figure of all of them, except maybe for the faces I don't know, and except—of course—for me.

The amazing thing is, in this collection of great legal minds, there isn't a single real card player. I watch them stumble and fumble around what should have been a pretty straightforward hand. These rough, tough faces are easy to read, easier than they suspect anyway. Petrovsky shows me his hole cards: nothing down, nothing up, a four-card straight with a hole in the middle of it. I can see what he's been doing, hanging around through a couple of rounds of cheap bets, just to see if the long-shot straight fills out.

I watch the others through the last face card. I'm trying to figure the game, I can't help it—and besides, it isn't that hard. Marinacci bets small, one of the faces folds, the others call right around to Petrovsky. He's about to call, too, but I lean in next to him before he can move and push in a stack of chips.

"Raise," I tell the table. "The professor raises."

Now the headlights are all back on, everybody but Petrovsky staring at me like it's sentencing time for the baby-killer. This strikes me as funny, for some reason. I don't know if I'm going to bring my legal career to a crashing halt before it even starts, but I just can't help myself.

Petrovsky whispers, out of the hearing of the others, "You're sure, Michael? I would have probably just called."

"You're good," I tell him.

"Okay," he says, his eyes full of doubt. "Raise it is."

It's a strange feeling, talking to him like this. Two days ago he was in the Unapproachable God category, but here, in this context, I can talk to him one-on-one. Maybe because here, on this ground, I know what I'm doing better than he does. Better than any of them.

The others call his raise, still pissed, then comes the last down card. Petrovsky doesn't make his straight. Marinacci is too grumpy to even make the five-dollar bet he started with last time.

"Check," he says.

Kaplan says, "Check to Martin and Lewis over there."

"Check to the raiser," says the district attorney, Shields, and the fourth face—I almost recognize him—says, "Czechoslovakia."

"What's the limit?" I ask the table.

"Twenty dollars," says Judge Marinacci. "The big bet is twenty dollars."

"Good," I say, shoving a pile of Petrovsky's chips into the pot. "Twenty-dollar bet for the professor."

This stirs them up again, all of them, especially the D.A., Shields.

"You've seen half the hand," he says. "How the fuck are you betting into us?"

Kaplan says, "Always the prosecutor, eh, Barry?"

The fourth face—Eisen is his name, Judge Eisen, it's coming to me slowly—says to Petrovsky: "You sure this is wise, Abe? It's your money the kid is betting with."

But this is my home ground. I know, they don't.

"It's plenty wise," I tell him. "Because we know what we're holding, and we *know* what you're holding."

Marinacci says, "The fuck you know what we all have."

"A summer clerkship in your office says I do."

I can feel myself getting a little bigger in his eyes, though he's not done being pissed off.

"I don't bet with jobs like that," he says. "Let's just say I'll put you at the top of the list if you're right."

"Okay," I tell him. "You were looking for that third three, but you forgot that this gentleman over here—"

"Professor Green," Petrovsky says.

"—that Professor Green folded it on Fourth Street and you're doing your best to represent that you have it. The D.A. made his two pair but he knows they're no good here. Judge Kaplan was looking to squeeze out that diamond flush, but he came up short. And Judge Eisen is futilely hoping that his queens will stand up. Like I said, the dean's bet is twenty dollars."

One by one, they all look into one anothers' faces; then, with a shake of the head or a shrug of the shoulders, they toss their hands into the muck until Petrovsky is the only man standing. He looks up at me, impressed, then—what the hell—collects his pot.

Eisen says, "What did you have, Abe?"

"Nothing but a busted straight."

This gets them all started again—like poking a stick into a wasp's nest except that this time there's an edge of respect, it feels like. These guys don't mind an honest con, especially if it works.

"All right, kid," Marinacci says. "Your first assignment: Pull up a seat next to me."

I'm tempted, all right. But I know what I'm supposed to be doing.

"I'd like to, Judge," I tell him, "but I don't play cards."

It's hard, I tell you, walking out on that game, especially walking out to do my time on the fucking truck. An open invitation to lay with those lambs—but I'm retired. The truth is I can always find games though. Easy games, tough games, straight games, crooked games, home games. I could turn the truck onto the Jersey Turnpike and be at the Taj in two hours.

Instead, half an hour after hanging out with the judges, I'm heading north into nowhere delivering baked goods. Mr. Ding-Dong to the rescue. Fuck the straight and narrow path, I think. It just gets straighter and narrower all the time. A little taste of action—a *little* taste, not even my cards, not even my money—and I'm ready to ditch this shit altogether, park the fucking truck by the side of the road somewhere, and head for the hills. I think about Jo and she's not even enough to keep me in it, not tonight. It's this: knowing that I don't have it. I don't want to go through life as a second-rate cardplayer. First-rate anything, I think. I want to do something that I am good enough for.

Something, that is, besides the fucking truck.

I got a late start, coming out of Petrovsky's office, and of course this is the one night where the truck won't start—the battery's dead on arrival, Knish can't be found, then we drive over half of New York trying to find an all-night auto parts store. I'm three-and-a-half hours late getting started.

It's quarter after nine by the time I get home the next morning. Jo's already up and dressed for work, hair and make-up, ready to go. I sit at the kitchen table, debating about whether I should open a beer or not.

"How'd it go?" she asks.

"Sick of that fucking route."

"You're almost done with it," she says. "A few more semesters, we'll both be reading our names on some firm's letterhead."

"I guess," I tell her.

"Anyway, I'm already late for work."

She leans down, gives me one of those Lucy-and-Ricky kisses, a " 'Bye, honey" special. What I've got in mind is a little more. I pull her down into my lap and start to kiss her neck.

"Come on, babe," she says. "Don't tempt me."

"Tempt you? I could hardly keep the truck on the road, thinking about you here all alone last night."

"Yeah?" she says. "You had to pull over? I want to hear every detail . . ."

I start whispering in her ear, giving her the details. I don't mind giving her the details.

She tries to wriggle free after a minute.

"Later," she says, flustered. "Tell me the rest later."

"Oh, this can't wait till later."

I pull her back down and then she's kissing me back and things start to get serious. She's doing a little more than kissing. Then, all of a sudden, it's over and she's standing next to me on the linoleum with a slightly dazed look on her face.

"I just don't have time, baby," she says.

"I'll be quick. You won't even feel a thing."

"We both know that's not true."

She looks at me, apologetic, then shifts and rearranges her outfit and she's all neat and professional again. I go to the sink, splash cold water on my face.

"I'm telling you, Jo," I say. "These long nights are killing me."

"They never used to."

"Those nights didn't seem long," I tell her. "Buy in at eight o'clock, look up and it's morning. Next thing you know, it's dark again."

I stop, remembering the little taste of action from last night, feeling the sudden hunger for it. Do I tell her about Marinacci or not? But she's going to find out sooner or later.

"You know what?" I say. "Something good did come out of last night. I think I'm hooked up for the summer."

"Hooked up how?"

"After I left you at the library, I impressed Judge Marinacci. Looks like I'm in line for a clerkship."

I can read the emotional weather in her eyes turn from friendly to suspicious.

"Hear me out now," I tell her. "The judges were playing cards and I read Marinacci's hand blind."

Cold front coming through. She doesn't like this one damn bit.

"So instead of coming home, you played cards with some judge?"

"No, no. I wasn't even playing. I just caught his eye by seeing through their cards. Now, as long as I don't fuck up moot court, the job'll be mine."

Pissed, she gathers her briefcase, ready to leave—then turns to me for one final salvo. She doesn't have a minute for sex but she's got all the time in the world for an argument.

"What job is that going to be?" she demands. "Writing opinions on high-stakes poker?"

"Come on, babe," I tell her, trying to calm her. "You're the one who told me I should bring my poker skills to the courtroom."

"What I meant was you should use your head—the way you read people, the way you can calculate odds on the spot. I didn't mean you should con your way into a summer job."

"Con?" I ask her. "I was networking."

Exasperated, she gives me a fuck-you look and heads for the door. But she can't quite help herself from launching one more rocket.

"You trying to con *me* now?" she asks. "Maybe you just don't get it. You'll be no different than those ex-college athletes—secure job with the D.A.'s office, as long as they never miss a Lawyer's League game. If you get in this way, Mike, you'll always be a hustler to them."

"I didn't even sit with them," I tell her. "I didn't even play."

It's much too late for anything to work though. She turns and marches out of the apartment, letting the door slam behind her.

Then I remember, and I go racing after her, running down the steps to catch her on the next landing.

"Hey, look," I say, "I hate to ask, but can I take the Jeep to-morrow?"

"Where to?"

"Worm is getting out," I tell her. This pleases her to no end. "I've got to pick him up."

"Tomorrow, beautiful."

"I promised I'd be there."

"Worm," she says, turning the word over in her mouth so she can feel how much she hates the taste of it. "I can't even believe you still know somebody called 'Worm.' "

"The guy's like my brother, Jo."

She looks at me—there you go—then gives me that little tilt to her head, she's-right-I'm-wrong. Then she's gone and I'm standing there alone in the hallway and somebody's baby starts to cry and the hallway smells like roach spray and I haven't been to sleep yet. And I didn't even play. I didn't even play.

Worm, though: It's hard to know what to feel about him getting out. It rains all the way down, a heavy spring storm off the Atlantic that the wipers can barely keep up with. The other cars break up into streaks and spatters of color. The rain and the cold, it takes me right back: to the smell of galoshes and rubber raincoats, linoleum, chalk dust, cafeteria food.

I met Worm—his real name is Les Murphy, but I'm the only person in the world that knows it—I met Worm at the Dwight Englewood Preparatory Academy over in Jersey. We were the only two scumbags attending. My father's office was there. It said CUS-TODIAN on the door. That's why they took me.

Worm's dad did the grounds, when he wasn't too fucking drunk. That's when we did them, me and Worm. Of course the grounds weren't all we did. Worm put us into a scam a day on all the young aristocrats we went to school with, selling dime bags of oregano, nunchakus, and firecrackers from Chinatown. Kept us in lunch money. One time we got the starting five to take a dive against Long Island Friends. Worm got tossed out over that one. The fucking point guard cracked.

Worm didn't though. I'd have been right out with him if he had.

So: a stand-up guy, as good a running buddy as you could ask for. On the other hand, as Jo would say—and she has said more than once—on the other hand, Worm is trouble. I don't know if it's him or me or some chemistry in the two of us when we're running together, but shit does tend to happen. Worm is wound up tight, tight. I make jokes about his dad, but mine was bad enough and his was way, way worse. I think back and it feels like a long time ago, but I can feel how all that shit was like the spring being wound up and that motor has been running ever since. Mostly, though, it's just a strong uneasy feeling that I've got all the way down to the state prison. It's that feeling of driving in the rain, moving without being able to see more than a few feet in front of you. It's that wondering how you got from your childhood to here.

The weather breaks by the time I get there, the sun comes out, one of those mornings where everything looks washed and clean. Maybe this will turn out all right. The prison yard does not look like a place where many good things happen—I sit in the Cherokee, surrounded by chainlink and razor wire, a stone guardhouse on either side of the double steel gate, waiting. Once in a while the guard looks out at me from the window of the gate. A face like an axe, he doesn't trust anybody. Once in a while a prisoner will walk by the fence inside the gate, staring out at me, at the free man—but always in a jumpsuit. It's never Worm.

I wait for half an hour past the time he said to meet him and I

41

wonder if he's going to stand me up. I wonder if he's made some new special fuckup that will keep him inside for longer, which would be typical. I am just about to pack it in and find some lunch, try back a little while later, when I catch a patch of black through the fences.

It's Worm, coming up to the gate, a guard at his side but free and easy. He's wearing what he always wears: black pants, black shoes, black slick hair, and a black leather jacket from the age of *Shaft*.

I get out of the car, walk up closer to the gate. I can see him flipping jokes at the gatehouse guard, at the escort. He doesn't care, he truly doesn't.

Then the green steel of the gate slides open, slowly, and Worm walks out a free man. He walks until he spots me, anyway, and then he breaks into double time and then he's all over me, hugging on me. It's weird to hug him like that but there's no other way to say it: I am no-doubt glad to see him again, no-doubt glad that he's out of the joint. Only that little whisper, that feeling that he could have stayed out of here with just a little more—what? A little more something. Whatever it is, he hasn't got it.

"Mike," he says, and squeezes me harder. He is a bony mother-fucker but strong as a monkey, those skinny little monkey arms. "I knew you'd be here, man," he says. "Never let me down, never."

I say, "I would have been here every month if you —"

"Nah. I didn't want you to see me like that."

"It's great to see you now, Corporal," I tell him. "It wasn't the same with you gone. They toughen you up any inside?"

We let each other go, and I back off and look at him: about ninety percent the same, but the changes aren't any good. He looks that much older, that much more tired. And the restlessness is still there. The spring is still unwinding.

Then I catch him again in a headlock, for only the five-thousandth time. Kids. Again I get that strange feeling of the cafeteria smell and the closed air of the school on a rainy day. It isn't nostalgia—that would mean I wanted to go back, which you couldn't make me—just the feeling that it's so close to me that I can hear and smell and taste it like I was still there.

Then Worm straightens, stiff-backed like a fighting cock. I follow his eyes to a jumpsuited inmate, walking the inside of the chainlink fence, escorted by a guard. He's a big man, black, a head taller than either me or Worm. It takes me a minute to see that he's giving us the finger with his outside hand, swinging it with his walk, casual.

"Hey, fuck you, too, Derald," Worm yells happily. "I'm out of here, man."

"I ain't going to dignify that," Derald says, not even breaking stride.

"I'm going to miss you," Worm says.

This is too much for Derald. He breaks the grip of the guard and races to the fence, close as he can get to Worm—not even pissed, not attack-dog but *serious*.

"You added insult to injury, man," Derald says. "You didn't have to do that. That shit is going to come back at you."

"Hey," Worm says. "Fuck you, Okay?"

Before Derald can answer, the guard has him in hand again. He goes without complaint but he looks back at Worm, twice, over his shoulder.

"What was that all about?" I ask Worm when he's gone out of sight again.

"Another satisfied customer," Worm says. "Let's go."

"You got anything?"

"Does it look like it?"

43

"Fuck you," I tell him, and lead him toward the car.

"Nice car," he says. "Looks like you're prospering."

"I borrowed it."

"Then get in your borrowed car and drive us far the fuck away from this place," he says. And we get in and it's just like always: me driving, Worm talking my fucking ear off, except that in Jo's Jeep you could hear yourself over the sound of the motor without having to shout.

"Check it out, man," he says, once we get out on the highway. He opens the little overnight bag he's got with him and in it are maybe a thousand cigarettes, in packs and cartons and just lying around loose.

"Richest motherfucker in Dannemora," he tells me. "That's why Derald was yelling at me—I took some serious capital out of the local economy."

"You couldn't cash them out?"

"Just where I was sitting when my time came up," he says. "I could have planned it better. You want one?"

"I'll take one for luck. I still don't light them."

"You better hope it's not Derald's fucking luck on this one," he says, handing me a Tareyton. He slips a cig into his own mouth, yanks the ashtray open, clicks the lighter down—a virgin ashtray as far as I know. Jo keeps it a no-smoking car. But I'm not about to tell Worm he can't light up. He would think of several things to say, starting with "pussy-whipped," and I don't want to hear any of them.

"So, I got three games going on a regular basis," he says, breathing around the smoke. "One with the *shvartzerim*, one with the *gringos*, and one with the hacks. And the trick is, I got to make enough cash in the white game to lose in the hack game. And I've got to trim enough smokes from the brothers to keep myself in the style to which I've become accustomed, without getting the shit kicked out of me."

"Tools?" I ask him.

He holds his empty hands in the air in front of him, turning them over like a magician.

I say, "Ah, *solo las manos.*"

"Painting's out of the question," he says. "Only an asshole would be holding evidence inside. Wait till you see what an artist I've become."

I laugh at this. Another thing about Worm: If he can't make me laugh, it's because I'm dead.

"You?" he asks.

"Forget about it. I don't mess with the railroad bible anymore."

"You're shitting me."

"I got cleaned out," I tell him. It still hurts to say it, especially to Worm: I got cleaned out.

"Mikey McDee?" Worm says. "I don't believe it."

"It was a real blood game, over at KGB's place."

"So the Mad Russian emptied your pockets?"

He's trying to be light about it but I can tell he's shook. He had plans for my money maybe. Worm has always got plans. We're driving out of the nice weather and back into the rain again and in the gray, cloudy light I can see the age on his face. The year inside has cost him a lot more than a year. It's weird to think of Worm as older or tired or worn but there he is.

"I didn't want to tell you while you were inside," I say. "Dispirit you like that."

He doesn't say anything, just starts fiddle-fucking around with the radio. The first fat drops come splashing down and I start the wipers again. Springsteen, rap, fucking country music, there's nothing good.

"So it's just law school now, huh?" he says, like I really have betrayed him. "What about money?"

"I'm driving Knish's truck."

"Jesus," he says. And for a moment he looks like he really is lost, like he doesn't know where he is or where he's going—a kind of blankness. It's a look I haven't seen before on him and I don't like it. Then, after a minute, he lights a cigarette and pulls himself out of it.

"Don't you worry, son," he says. "The cavalry is here."

"Don't even think about it," I tell him. "I'm not playing. I'm done."

Worm laughs at this.

"Sure you're done," he says. "Just like you were done flipping baseball cards in junior high after you lost them all. Like you were done with women when Chrissy Rapoza left you blue-balled that whole weekend down the shore." He squares his shoulders toward me, pointing his cig at my face. "Now, listen," he says, "I know a game—a real berry patch just outside the city."

"Well, I'll drop you," I tell him.

Worm gives me a look like he almost believes me, then settles back to watch the smoke from his cigarette drift through the air, around the car and then out through the cracked window. It's raining, four o'clock.

He can't stop, I think. There's no other life for him, nothing coming after this. It's weird: I've only had a future for a couple of years now but I've really gotten attached to the idea. By now I'm starting to wonder if this was really a good idea, to come pick him up. It's a fight with Jo, sure thing. Plus this shit where he knows me better than I know myself is irritating. It's a problem with old friends: they don't believe you can ever change, they think you're the same person you were in the sixth grade, forever. I want to tell him, Look, you don't know me—who I am, what my life is like. But there's no way to say it, and he wouldn't believe me anyway.

A couple of hours, I tell myself. Drive him to the game and then I'll see him again in a month or two. It's what you do.

It's eight-thirty when I get him to his game. By the time we get to Princeton, New Jersey, the inside of the car is ankle-deep in junk food wrappers and blue with smoke, and Worm and I have figured out where we are again—in trouble with Jo, I think, as always. But this is minor trouble. I am going to be a good boy and stay out of the big trouble. Worm has got his setup and I am going to leave it to him.

"See, I know this girl named Barbara," he tells me. "She's the hostess at this eating club."

"Which is what?"

"What?"

"An eating club," I tell him. "What's an eating club? It sounds dirty."

"You wish," he says. "No, it's this thing they got at Princeton, you know, it's like a private club for college kids. Rich kids, you know? You've got to be invited to join."

"So how did you get an in?"

"Like I say, this girl Barbara works there." He opens the glove compartment, strains to read a little handwritten map by the light inside. "She is a piece of work, our Barbara is. Fucking nice-looking. Looks like the girl next door. Take a right, next big street."

"And?"

"And what?"

"What about Barbara?"

"I don't mess with junkie chicks," he says. "You think I'm going out with her? This is a business deal—I'm her cousin from out of town. I never played poker before. That's all."

47

"Whatever you say," I tell him. It's the one area where I expect Worm to lie to me, his sex life, and as near as I can tell he does all the time. I couldn't ever tell you who he was interested in or what he was interested in or why. I quit asking a long time ago, which doesn't keep him from bringing it up.

The rain has tapered off but it still drips down from the trees—old trees, expensive trees, trees standing in deep green lawns in front of big old houses. It's still light enough to make out the size of these places, big old boxes. The lights are on inside, yellow and warm. In our old neighborhood, you'd walk along this time of night and every house would be lit up by the TV, a flickering shadowy blue. Not in Princeton. This is what education can do for you apparently. I wonder what a law degree from City Law will do for me. Not this, I know: you had to be born to this.

"This is the street," Worm says. "Left here and up four houses."

"Nice neighborhood," I tell him.

"Nothing but nice around here," he says. "Nothing but money. Mother of shit, would you look at that place?"

Waterton Lodge sits off from the street on what looks like ten acres of lawn, a rambling old-brick pile with turrets and porches and arches. It starts a little fear in me, just looking at it. This isn't Worm's kind of place. This is Indian country for him and me. Worse for him; Jo's taught me enough of the language to get by, enough of the manners. Look out, buddy, I think. These people are soft, but not as soft as you think. Not all of them anyway.

"Nice hook up," I tell him.

"Pretty damn nice," he says. "Only one problem. I got this feeling?"

"Which feeling is that exactly?"

"You know the feeling," Worm says. "You got your table all set . . ."

48

"Yeah."

"You got your knife and fork . . ."

"Uh-huh."

"You got your sauce there, your A-1 and your Luger's . . ."

"The only thing missing is the stake," I say, filling in the punch-line. I reach down into my pants pocket and pull out my money clip.

"Exactly," Worm says. "A nickel should get me started."

A nickel: I wish. I peel a hundred off the top, Worm watching like a hungry dog, but after that is only twenties.

"Damn," Worm says. "How you living?"

"A little light. I told you. Anyway, I've got two hundred and twenty dollars for you."

"Shit," Worm says. "That's only eleven big bets. Not even enough to establish table image."

"Good, so forget this game. I'll straighten you out tomorrow in the city."

"Need to get started tonight," Worm says. "I'm already behind."

"You just got out, what's the fucking hurry?"

"The hurry," he says. "What's the hurry? At least five guys been waiting on my release."

The way he says it is like the way I told him about my night at Teddy's: it's hard to get the words out, hard to get your lips to move right. It's just so fucking embarrassing, for one thing. Makes me think he's in worse trouble than I know about.

"How much you owe?" I ask him.

"Over ten," he says. "Can't even figure the juice." He stops and stares at the skinny bankroll again, the same hungry dog. "Two-twenty," he says. "Damn. Maybe a *cardplayer* could get something going with two hundred and twenty dollars . . ."

Now his cards are on the table: the running-buddy angle, the flattery, the old hard luck, and so on. It's not like I don't want to help. I just don't want to get hustled out of a thing I worked hard to get.

"I heard you asking in the car," I tell him, "and I hear you now, but I can't do it. I just can't do it. I've made promises."

"Okay," Worm says. Something closes up in his face then. I get the public face, the cheerful anything-goes. "I understand," he says. "I respect that, and it's all right and I'll be fine. I'll just have to make some moves early that might play better to a later audience . . . not the first time."

I hand him the money and he takes it, like he was taking it from a stranger.

"Premium hands, buddy," I tell him, and I mean it.

"I'll make sure of it," he says.

He shakes my hand, lets himself out of the car, and heads for the Waterton lodge, a boxer's step in his walk. He's ready; or at least he's got the front. Halfway there he turns back to me.

"And Mike?" he says.

"Yeah?"

"It's great to see you, man."

A last wave—hand open, fingers stretched out wide—and then he turns back toward the lodge.

I start off down the road again: the thick, dripping greens and trees, the rich houses. Somewhere at the other end of this is my apartment, where Jo will be waiting or not. It's a long-ass drive and it makes me tired to think about it and it makes me tired to think about Worm. I tell myself that he'll do fine in the game. I tell myself that he's got my whole bankroll, pitiful as it is. I tell myself that he's my friend, and that I'm doing right by him.

But I'm not stupid.

Leaving him there, miles from nowhere, that's the end of something. Then the question is whether it's something that needs end-ing, and that I don't know. I kick it around, driving north toward the turnpike. On the one hand, on the other hand. I'm not the same guy I was in tenth grade and maybe it's time I stopped acting like it. I have furniture now. I have a girlfriend, a future. I don't need Worm to fuck it up.

On the other hand, he's having more fun than I am.

Also: maybe I'm just chickenshit. Maybe I let that whipping from Teddy KGB take a little too much out of me. I don't know. But when I think about that game at Princeton, I hear this little scared voice saying maybe I don't have it anymore, maybe I won't be able to take them.

And this last is what decides it: I turn the car around, ten miles out of Princeton, and head straight back for the Waterton Lodge. I'm not going to let any little voices push me around. Fuck you, I think—nondirectionally, you know, just everything in my way. Fuck it, fuck you, here I come. Still, I've got that little raggedy doubt. It pesters me all the way back. Jack King, the guy who wrote *Confessions of a Winning Poker Player*, says that nobody can remember the big pots they won but every player can remem-ber the outstanding tough beats of his career. Something like that. The thing I remember about it specifically is the words *outstand-ing tough beats*, which stuck with me. They echo and repeat in my brain as I head back for the lodge, one of those phrases you can't get out of your head: outstanding tough beats, outstanding tough beats, outstanding tough beats.

I've got one bill, a single hundred, folded up and tucked inside a pack of cigarettes. I fish it out, unfold it; then I take one of the cigarettes out and put it in my mouth, just for luck. I don't light it. I can hardly remember how I built my bankroll, but I can't stop thinking of how I lost it.

Inside is like a hotel, a really good hotel in midtown: dark wood paneling, oil paintings of horses, fresh flowers on the tables. All the furniture is a hundred years old at least. I don't belong here. This whole room is designed to let me know I don't belong here. Fuck you, I think, you and you and you: the clean rich college kids, laughing and talking. You think you know but you don't know.

"You must be Mike," says the hostess, coming around the end of her walnut desk to take my arm: the famous Barbara. She's beautiful but she doesn't have the look, her hair's jet black and there's too much olive in her skin, too much Italy or Spain. She smiles and lights the place up.

"Worm said you'd be joining him," she says. "Come with me."

She leads me through the dining room, arm in arm, and all the time I'm thinking about Worm and whether he's conning me. But of course he's conning me. What else would he be doing? That's what he does instead of breathing. No, the question is whether I'm letting go of too much of myself by going along with him, and that's a question I don't have an answer for. We pass by table after table of the young and the white and the beautiful, and I think: I could be one of them. I'm scheduled to be. But here I am on the other side again . . .

Barbara leads me into a dark hallway off the main dining room, down a narrow passage.

"I'm not here to play," I tell her. "Just keep company."

The bland, friendly look falls from her face and I see the hard edge of Barbara, the hungry little schemer.

"No, no, that's no good," she says. "See, here's the play: you're my new boyfriend, looking for a regular game."

"Really, I'm not much of a card player."

She stops cold in the hallway, gives me a look: she's tired of my bullshit. There isn't time.

"Worm told me that's precisely what you are," Barbara says. "My cut's twenty-five percent."

"I see," I tell her; and she stands there a minute longer, searching my face to see whether Worm has put her on to another bad deal again. I don't give her anything. She can make up her own mind.

She composes herself into the bland look again before she leads me into the back room—some kind of den or smoking room or some such shit, smaller and darker and richer even than the main room. No fresh flowers here; instead, five boys in tweed and LL Bean and khaki and, right in the middle of them, Worm. In his leather jacket and prison skin, he stands out.

"Gentlemen," Barbara says. "This is my boyfriend Michael."

Friendly smiles, half-waves, and murmured hellos: everybody's so fucking *nice*. Plus they're trying to figure me out, I imagine. I'm dressed more or less like one of them but I'm not fooling anybody, is my bet. Good enough for Barbara anyway.

"Be nice to him," she says. "Leave him enough to buy me breakfast."

She gives me a big warm kiss—a little too warm for the club boys but I don't mind. I can smell her perfume and the shampoo in her hair and feel her body up against mine and it's a good body, round and generous, none of this skinny-woman stuff. And then I think of Jo, the skinny woman, and how this is all fake: Barbara's a junkie, at least according to Worm. I have this feeling that I'm selling out something real to chase after something fake, smoke and mirrors, the dream of the perfect hustle.

"Good luck, honey," Barbara says, and trails her hand out of mine as she leaves, just like it was for real, like we were in love.

I sit down at the table, buy in with my much-folded hundred. The club boys introduce themselves but only a couple of the names stick: Birch, a blond kid with bad zits, looks like he was raised in a cave, and Higgins, the super-preppie. Horn-rims, big hair, and a tweed sportcoat. He looks like the cartoon version of a Princeton boy and I wonder, for a moment before I get to work, whether he's for real or whether he's putting on an act, too. It doesn't seem impossible.

Worm is dealing: "The game's Chicago."

"You know Chicago?" Birch asks.

"Remind me," I say.

"Stud game," Birch says, using that manly voice to show he knows what he's doing. He's tough, all right. "High spade in the hole wins half the pot."

I nod earnestly, trying to stick all these complicated rules in my memory. The antes go in and Worm deals the hole cards, then the first face card. I take a look in the hole, half expecting what I see there: jack of hearts, ace of spades.

Fucking Worm.

The thing is, I don't need his help with these fish. I could be blind, crippled, and crazy and still make money at this table. It's insulting, almost—the idea that I need mechanics to take them down. It does make things go quicker though. I take my half of the first pot, skip a couple, win a couple, nothing too high-profile. About half an hour in, I tip off an obvious bluff and Higgins chases me down on it, and from that point on, I'm the sucker who doesn't know anything. Worm, they're a little suspicious of—you'd have to be blind not to be suspicious—but he's losing slowly and steadily. No problem with Uncle Worm. After a while, this starts to feel like fun.

Worm and I fall into our old rhythm like Clyde Frazier and Pearl

Monroe. We bring out all the old-school tricks. Stuff that would never play in the city—signaling, chip placing, trapping, we even run the old best-hand play. Like I say, I could crack this game just as quickly straight up, but there's no risk in this room. Some people might look down on Worm's mechanics, call it immoral, but as Canada Bill Jones said, It's immoral to let a sucker keep his money.

Like they teach you in One-L: caveat emptor, pal.

One of the LL Bean boys decides that I am visible, halfway through a hand.

"Are you at university, Michael?" he asks.

Birch checks.

"No, I go to law school in New York," I tell him. "Raise fifty."

"Call," Higgins says, nudging his big chips toward the pot. "Columbia?"

"City Law," I tell him. "Night."

"Call," says one of the others—curly hair, glasses, I never got his name. "Night?" he says. "You must be quite industrious."

I give him my best salesman's smile, you bet.

"Call," Birch says.

"I guess my pedigree wasn't as spotless as all yours," I tell him. "I'm full."

I flip the hand—queens full of sixes—and feel the little sag go around the table. They knew they could beat me, every one of them. They *knew* it.

And maybe, just maybe, on a good day they might have been right once in a while. Not with Worm at the table though. Not as long as you let him touch the cards. He has really become an artist: Discard Culls, Pickup Culls, Overhand Runups, the Double Duke, his techniques is flawless. Half the time I miss it myself, and I know exactly what to look for. The college boys are like kids at a magic show: presto change-o your money is gone-o!

Worm's technique is perfect but his judgment is a little off. A few times I have to fold the case hand just so it won't be obvious. Too many rabbits are showing up in too many hats. Even these boys might start to notice. The thing that puts it over on them, though, is the fact that Worm is losing steadily and stupidly throughout the evening. He plays the part of the loser to perfection: going deep on two pair, grinning like he can't help himself at the sight of his good hand. You might suspect him of a mild case of Down's syndrome but you'd never think he was outsmarting your ass.

Hand after hand, he goes down a little, I go up a little, the river of cards carrying us all along. The college boys don't notice the shift, the way their money is slowly migrating from in front of them into my stack. It's nice, it's easy, it's friendly, everybody but Worm. Chip by chip, dollar by dollar he's going broke. It's ten-thirty by the time he bets the last of his chips on a little straight.

He gets beat by a flush.

He kicks his chair back from the table with an angry jerk, and addresses the table: "Like my Uncle Murphy says: When the last dime is gone, it's time to move on," he says. "Thanks a fucking lot, guys. I'm outta here."

This is bad manners. The boys react by shutting up, a general silence that holds until one of them can think of the correct response. It's the one who looks like he's about to go hiking that speaks for all of them.

"Come back anytime," the boy says. "Your money's always good here."

Worm grins at him, obviously trying to figure whether or not to jump on the guy and tear his throat out. A little thrill of fear runs around the table: he's pissed, he's broke, he's not one of us, look out! There's no telling what a boy from the lower classes might do. I try to look scared myself. Really this is pretty enjoyable to watch, one of Worm's better performances.

Finally he spins on his heel and takes off, leaving a general relief, a little worried giggling. From here on out, I'm on my own. But I am up to the job. I work and I work and I work, trying to keep them in the game. Money changes hands, theirs to mine, and the hard part is trying to hold their interest. What's holding them there? Pride, mostly—nobody wants to be the first one to call it a night—and the faint forlorn hope of getting some of their money back. Or maybe it's just a way of passing the time, I think. Maybe the money doesn't matter so much, maybe it's worth it to drop a couple of hundred just to stave off the colossal boredom of their regular lives. Maybe this is the high wire for them, the thing that makes it worth it.

Or maybe they're just too dumb to know when they've been beat.

By one in the morning, it's over. The super-preppie, Higgins, runs himself out of money in three stupid hands and there is nothing I can do to keep him in the game. And once he's quit, the others don't need an excuse anymore. I stay in character while we pack up the cards, sort out the money—and I try to seem as surprised as everybody else at what it adds up to, my oh my. It's always a crucial moment, when the numbers get added up, but these boys seem to weather it all right. I just don't want any bad feeling—and then I realize that the reason why is that somewhere in the back of my mind, I'm planning to come back. I might need these boys again. It's the old habit of hustling and it seems to be alive again. I think back to last night, last week, last month on the truck, and it seems like a long time ago. More than that: it seems like somebody else's life, somebody else's trouble. I didn't really mean to let that cat out of the bag.

It's dark when we get out into the hallway, dark and quiet. We're the last people in the place and Barbara is waiting up for us, the good little servant girl.

"How'd you do, honey?" she asks, fetching the boys their coats. She hands them over the counter and then comes to stand next to me, the girlfriend, I remember. I slip my arm around her shoulders and remember that feeling again, good and warm. And for that moment I let myself forget that it's fake. I won, says the little voice inside. I beat them all.

"Your boyfriend's lucky in love and lucky in cards," says Birch, the one with the zits. "He won every hand there at the end."

One of his pals laughs at this, grumpy. "Just the hands he played, Birch. I'm going home—I've got an eight o'clock tomorrow."

They slip their coats on, out of gas suddenly, run-down, while I've got that winning feeling in my chest, eight feet tall and bulletproof. I feel like pushing it; and I do.

I look Barbara in the eyes and say, "The only bad thing about cards is it keeps me away from you, sweetheart."

I can see the anger in her eyes—it's her ass more than mine if we get caught somehow—but I don't care. I'm just running with the feeling. Not that any of them notice anyway. They get their parkas on, dressed for the mountains again, and we go out in a cluster to the parking lot. Good night, good night. Nobody feels like hanging around. I lean against Barbara's car, my arm around her, watching them go. I can feel her breath, her warmth. Hard to believe that she's in the kind of trouble Worm says she is.

Then I remember the hungry, hard look on her face, taking me into the game, and I believe.

When everybody's gone, she drops out of my arm like a wrestling hold and knocks on the roof of her car.

Worm pops up from the backseat, a jack-in-the-box in a leather jacket. He gets out of the car, grinning, and says, "Cut up the green."

Oh, does he love a hustle. And, for now, I do, too—but Barbara's unhappy again, and hungry. She watches my hands as I count out the wad, separating the twenties, tens, and fives, straightening the heads—Franklin, Lincoln, Jackson—so they all go the same direction. Everybody loves them dead presidents. It's a little over fifteen hundred altogether, a very nice night's work in this kind of shallow water. I fold my little hundred back together, count out the original two-twenty, then count out Barbara's.

"Yours is three hundred," I tell her.

She takes the money from my hand, trying to be cool and slow but the greed comes out as she counts it, the little frantic movements. Three hundred: she counts it again. I don't know why I would cheat her.

"Thank you, boys," she says, satisfied.

Worm says, "When can we see you again?"

She says, "Give it a few—"

But I break in: "No no," I tell them, both of them. "I'm done. This one was just, just because."

Barbara looks from Worm to me to Worm. He's the one who will tell her what I'll do. He just shrugs his shoulders.

"All right, then," Barbara says. Whatever. She gets in her car—a battered Nova, a white-trash car—starts it on the third try and drives away in a cloud of oil smoke, leaving the two of us. It's well after midnight, way out in New Jersey. We lean up against the hood of the car for a second, the night's work done, just getting ready to go. Worm lights a cigarette. The clouds are hanging low in the sky, but they're white, instead of the dirty pink they turn in the city. Even the sky is better in Princeton. The rich can afford a better class of sky.

"How'd you know I'd come?" I ask Worm.

This cracks him up.

"Josey Wales," he says. "The Preacher. The Man with No Name. Clint always doubles back when a friend's in need."

He reaches his hand out toward me, blind, expecting me to slap him a soft five. But I don't know—I suddenly feel like all this buddy-movie stuff is not for me. It's from the eighth grade, it feels like. It's dumb, as in dumb-on-purpose. Don't get me wrong, I'm not above it. But suddenly the good feeling in my chest is gone, evaporated. I take the keys to the Jeep and drop them into Worm's outstretched palm.

"You drive," I tell him.

orning: or something like it. We get to the parking garage at quarter to seven and the city is already awake, the taxis rolling, the vendors setting up tables on the sidewalk. I've got this feeling, King of the World—or what's left of it anyway. Parts of me are scattered from here across New Jersey but I'm not one of these people going to work.

Except I ought to be.

Lots of things for me to do. I don't need Jo to remind me. I don't want to let go of the feeling, though, the high. All the way back up I was dreaming of Las Vegas again, the big time, the high life. Now it's morning and I've got things to do—a meeting, I remember. The moot court team. Nine o'clock.

"We made nice time," Worm says. "Breakfast?"

"Nah," I tell him. "I have to fucking get home—if Jo hasn't

61

changed the locks on me. And I barely have time for a shower before this meeting."

"Come on," he says. "I'll pick the lock for you. I'm thinking waffles, egg sandwich. I'm buying."

"Save your money for once. I can't. I'll see you later."

"At least you could straighten me out before you go?"

I don't want to, not right then—I need to get home, get ready, get back into my life. But I don't want the furniture looking at me, not yet. I don't want to let go.

"All right," I tell him. "I'll skip the shower. Come on."

We walk over crosstown, away from the river and New Jersey and toward the Chesterfield. People are working by the river—people sweeping, moving garbage, fixing cars—but by the time we get over to Madison everything's quiet again. The club is on a side street, out of the flow of traffic. Right before we go in there's one of those weird moments you get sometimes in the morning, when by some accident everything stops at once, and it's quiet for a second, maybe two seconds, and you hear what it would sound like if it was quiet.

It's spooky. It even seems to get to Worm. He looks up and down the outside of the building where the club is.

"Here?" he says. "Real carpet joint, huh?"

"Listen," I tell him, one hand on the doors. "This may not look like Teddy's place, but this ain't the Ivy Leagues, either. You can't fuck up around here. You've got to play on your belly."

"Sure," Worm says. " 'Course, chief." But I can tell he isn't paying attention. He's highstepping like a racehorse, edgy, wanting the action. I let him through the doors, knowing I'm making a mistake. I stop him again on the stairs, try to explain.

"I'm serious," I tell him. "You know I got nothing against the

62

way you help yourself. But the guys here are fast company. They'll spot every move, and you won't just get a finger up your spine."

"Fine, already," Worm says, impatient. "Fine."

He's dancing from foot to foot, he's ready. For a minute I think I ought to blow him off, let him find his own fucking game, but that would take longer. I'm already late. I just don't think Worm's a good match for the Chesterfield is all.

But by then we're at the door and it's too late. The electronic eye of the camera in the corner picks me up, the little video friend, and whoever it is behind the counter must recognize me: the door clicks open.

It's Petra: tall, dark, beautiful in a kind of outrageous way—I mean, she points her tits at you first, you notice them, and you're off to the races. I have mixed feelings about this. We gave each other a try for a while, so all this freelance sex she radiates in every direction makes me jealous, although I have no right and no real reason. Also, she knows better then this. She's got a big brain in there. But this is what she does.

She looks good anyway, despite the hardwired panic button that dangles around her neck. She's already standing when I come in, from seeing me in the monitor. She comes around the counter to shake my hand.

"Michael McDermott," she says. "How are you doing, Mike?"

She looks at me. We have a moment in which we're both trying to say something with our eyes but I don't know what. I can't help drifting down to the body under her dress, which I am supposed to.

She says, "The computer tried to delete you last week, but I knew you'd be back."

"Well, I'm not," I tell her, which she doesn't believe. "It's good to see you, Petra. This is Les Murphy, he's like my brother."

Worm pushes himself forward.

"Call me Worm," he says, and shoves his hand out toward her. He wants to win all the money *and* sleep with all the women, and probably run for president besides.

"Hey," says Petra dubiously, looking from Worm's face to mine and back, questioning. But then the phone rings behind the counter, and she walks off to answer it. She doesn't run, she wouldn't run. A very cool young woman.

Worm is taking in the Chesterfield, ogling it: a big-screen TV in the corner with ESPN going, no sound. Couches, coffee tables, lamps, and carpeting. There's even a pool table in the corner, not that I have ever seen anybody take a shot on it, or watch the TV, or sit on the couches. People come here to play, the rest is just decoration. There are six or eight tables sitting empty and just the one going, off in the corner. It's nice, but it's not that nice. Still it's enough to impress Worm.

"What's with the necklace on her?" he asks, nudging his head toward Petra.

"They're wired right into the precinct," I tell him. "They got 'em on the payroll."

Worm lets out a low, almost inaudible whistle. He likes it here. Which he ought to: yesterday at this time he was in the cooler. Now he's loose on the unsuspecting world. I don't know—I still don't think he understands that all this furniture doesn't make the people any softer or any nicer or any better to put shit over on.

Petra finishes her call—some small definite business—and comes back around the counter to join us. She seems to be glad to see me, in her opaque way. Maybe she's glad to see me and maybe she hates my guts. I'll never know.

"What are they playing?" I ask her, angling my head toward the game in the corner.

"Twenty-forty forced rotation is the only game going right now," she says.

"Is that fat Greggie sitting twenty-forty now?" I ask her. "The game's that soft?"

"Yeah, it's a real live game. Are you guys going to play?"

I can see Worm out of the corner of my eye, practically salivating. And I wouldn't mind myself: there is money on the table and money to be made. And I've still got the good feeling from last night, somewhere in my chest—the *certainty*, the dead flat knowledge that I could take this game.

"Have a seat, Mike," says Worm. It must be showing on me, how much I want it. Or maybe he really does know me, better than I know myself. "We'll take this room apart."

I can't help one more look over at the table. When I see the action, I'm not tired anymore, I'm not dirty, I've got nowhere to go but here and nothing to do but this. And I *know* I could take them. I know I could.

"It's not going to happen," I finally say to Worm. "I told you, one time thing. I'm off it, man."

"Fucking shame," Worm says—to Petra, not to me. He's already moved beyond me, on to the next game, the next step. To me he says, "All right—go running home to her."

"Sure, Worm, I will. Take care of him, Petra."

She gives me one last unreadable glance and buzzes me out, behind the solid walnut of her counter again. Worm follows her, drawn to the action. For him, I'm gone before I leave the room. I'm gone the minute I say no to the game. I can hear him talking on my way out: "Girl's got a hold of them, I guess . . ."

The steel door slams shut behind me and I'm outside and it's morning again. Fucking Worm, I think. Juvenile bastard, stuck in the sixth grade for life. But he's the one inside, he's the one in that soft twilight of smoke and cards and coffee where it all runs together. He's playing.

While I'm out on the street. I hurry back to the apartment, already late, brushing against the city as it wakes up, the daylight taking over. The daylight self counts off the various offenses of the night: two women, Barbara and Petra, were looked at or touched with sex in mind; the Cherokee had been smoked in; cards had been played; money had been won; the life of the law, the good life, the straight life, had been held in contempt, had almost been given up, in fact. And here, on the sidewalk, I think about the nights I wasted on that fucking truck and I know that I'm not going back. This is a scary thought, one I didn't mean to have. But once you think it, you can't unthink it. The toothpaste won't go back in the tube.

So: I'm done with the truck.

What's next? I'm tired all of a sudden, too tired to figure it out. Something will happen and something will happen after that. I don't know. I can't tell from here.

Seven-thirty. I try to tiptoe into the apartment, shoes off by the front door and into the bedroom when I realize Jo is sitting at the kitchen table already, still in her bathrobe but showered and awake, a cup of coffee on the table in front of her.

She says, "Reunion run a little late?"

"Couldn't call," I tell her. "Didn't want to wake you."

I put my hand on her shoulder, trying for the familiar, trying for touch. But she flinches away, right away. She doesn't want any part of it.

"I wasn't sleeping, Mike," she says. This is going to be a fight, but not right now. "Anyway, change quick, we'll share a cab."

"Know what?" I tell her. "Go ahead without me. I need a

shower. You can cover for me if I miss a little of the Mulligan meeting."

Okay: I'm trying to hustle her, it's true. I've got a couple of secrets. But it's nothing major, I did walk away. And there's nothing to be gained by talking about it. Hurt feelings, noise. I take my jacket off and drape it over a kitchen chair, same as always. Nothing's wrong, nothing to look at here.

"At least give me a story," she says. She is not falling for any of it. "Tell me you were out drinking till you threw up. Tell me you were getting lap dances over at Scores. Tell me some fucking thing."

"That's right, Jo, I was out entertaining Worm."

"Uh-huh."

"What can I say?" I ask her, but she's got her prosecutor's face on. "I owed it to him," I tell her.

She makes a face and stands up to leave. Then a glimpse of mercy, unexpected: she decides to give me a chance.

"So you were nowhere near a card game?" she asks.

All I have to do is say no.

She's watching my face. She thinks, like a lot of women do, that she can tell if I'm lying or not, that she can see it in my eyes. She's forgetting that I'm good at this—I'm in practice. When I'm good, I don't even let myself know if I'm lying or not. See, I wasn't even really in that game, it was Worm's game. And it was a one-time thing certainly, and I did walk away from the Chesterfield this morning. Telling her all about the greasy little details of last night would really screw her head up and screw things up for me and it wouldn't even be an accurate picture of what went on. It would just be a lot of mess about nothing. The truth is that I'm cool and I'm clean, and I don't want to give her a bunch of little misleading facts that might distract her from this.

"No," I tell her. And she believes me.

Or maybe she decides to believe me. There's a difference. She comes over and gives me a hug, but it's not one of the warm kind.

"Okay, then," she tells me, without quite looking at me. "Shower quick, I'll wait for you, we'll go to the meeting together."

And that's that; or it ought to be. I go into the bedroom, strip off my clothes—the smoke and sweat makes them feel like I've been wearing them for a week—and step naked into the shower. I feel like weeks and months of sin are steaming off me in there, feel like I'm coming clean. All the shit is stripping off me, all the failure grease from Knish's truck, all the teenage vice with Worm. I'm going to get out of there a new man, which is good: I was getting tired of the old one, who wasn't either one thing or the other, who was always in the middle, always halfway between. Worm is Worm, at least. You can't take that away from him. And Jo is Jo and so on. It's only me that's always in the middle like this—or used to be. Not anymore. One person, one life. That's what I'm thinking, standing there under the hot water. No more in-between.

I hear Jo come in while I'm showering, and I call out to her. I'm happy, for some reason. I want to tell her, though I actually don't want to tell her anything. I just want to talk.

But she doesn't hear me. That's what I think at the time—she must have come in to get some makeup or something, some vital girl ingredient, and gone out without hearing me. When I come out of the shower, though, I find out I was wrong.

When I come out of the shower, my roll is sitting there on the edge of the sink, my gambler's roll of hundreds and twenties bound up with a rubber band. Dirty, guilty money. I am busted. I call her name in the empty apartment but I already know: she's gone, gone, gone.

an hour later, of course, I'm sitting across the table from her at the moot court meeting. Not that she's exactly letting her eyes rest on me.

She's explaining the world to Kelly and Griggs when I walk up: "The most important thing to remember is to be respectful to the judges, but not obsequious—"

"Wait a minute," Kelly says. She's a straight little button, dresses like a Catholic high school girl but smart, easy to underestimate. "Make sure to be deferential."

"Gene Marinacci won't buy deferential," I tell them, setting my briefcase on the table, letting myself into the group. Kelly looks at me like something that crawled out from under the sink while Jo is looking right through me.

"Oh, I see. It's 'Gene,' is it?"

This is Griggs, the fourth member of our little team, and apparently the only one who can stand me right now. He says, "I knew there was a reason you were lead counsel, and it's got nothing to do with your punctuality."

"Sorry," I say lamely, and sit down. "I couldn't find a cab."

This apparently is annoying enough to Jo that she lets me see, just for a second, how pissed off she is. What? I don't know—just the greasy smell of cafeteria food, the zero sleep, something, makes me feel like it's all lost and gone and I'm just wasting my time here. I sit down anyway. Nothing else to do.

"Fine," Jo says, keeping her eyes in careful midair, nowhere near me. "So when you give the opening remarks, be sure to stip to the fact pattern, and make sure you have the right cites. Use book cites not Lexis . . ."

She trails off, for no reason. Then I see that there's something behind me shuts her up. I follow her eyes and there is Knish, standing two feet behind me and grinning like he's on acid.

"I don't mean to interrupt you future magistrates and noblemen, but I need a word," he says. "Hey, Jo, long time."

She looks from his face to mine and back: two assholes.

"How are you, Knish?" she says, daring him to answer.

"You need to talk?" I ask him.

"It's important."

I look at Griggs, and Kelly, and Jo: I might as well go. They don't seem to have any particular use for me at this point. I overhear Kelly, on the way out of the room, talking to the others: "I'll act as lead counsel," she says. The old Alexander Haig trick: Don't nobody worry, I'm in charge here.

The smile drops from Knish's face as soon as we get out into the hall.

"What are you thinking?" he asks me, pissed.

"What the hell are you talking about?"

"You're leaking all over the place, Mikey," Knish says. "You're on tilt. How could you bring this guy, this *Greek dealer*, down to the club?"

Suddenly I'm aware that any of the other students could be listening, any of the dozens passing by, that any of this might make interesting news in the law school. The two halves of my life are collapsing on each other. I couldn't keep them apart after all. This isn't going to end well, it can't.

"Look," I tell him, "we can't talk here."

I lead him out of the building, away from the eyes, away from that other life where he doesn't have any part. We go over across the street, a little park with a couple of benches, and all the while Knish is talking about what an asshole Worm is.

"The guy's a cheat," Joey says. "He always has been. Right now he's over there at Chesterfield's ruining your reputation with every lousy second he deals."

"Shit," I say. I wish I was a little more surprised. This is the thing that Worm is missing, the thing that's supposed to tell him when to stop. Again I feel this heaviness settle into my chest, knowing that all I can do to help him isn't going to be enough. I fish a cigarette out of my pocket, stick it in my mouth.

"I told him," I say to Knish. "Anybody else see?"

"Nobody saw," Knish says. "I heard it. The snapping sound gave it away. If I didn't know him, I might not have noticed. But I turn around and see him there with that mechanic's grip, and I know."

"Did you give him the office?"

"Yeah, I tried to warn him but he looked right through me."

"Shit," I say again. This is Worm all right. That boy could fuck up a wet dream. And part of me doesn't mind going to the rescue. Part of me would rather face an angry Worm and a tableful of pissed-off poker players than go back in that cafeteria and talk law with my dog-faced team. At least I know what I'm doing here. I mean, I know what I'm doing with Jo and the law school, too—I just can't seem to stay on the right side of it. With Worm, things are a little easier.

This strikes me as a bad sign about myself.

"I better go get him," I tell Joey.

"Sit a while," he says, gesturing me down onto the bench next to him. "He's okay now. Most of those Georges are on the tail end of a thirty-six-hour session and they can't see straight. But if he's still there when Roman and Maurice start their game, he's going to wish he was still inside."

"No," I say, still standing. Roman and Maurice are Russian mob guys, one step down from Teddy KGB but still, you don't want to cross them. I can see Worm walking right into this one. I say, "I got to go get him."

"I understand," Knish says, shrugging elaborately. "I understand."

I leave him there on the bench—ready to feed the pigeons, from the looks of him—and head downtown, hoping that Worm will still be in one piece when I get there. Midtown, midday: the only quick way is the train, so I duck down underground, out of the daylight. The waiting is the hard part. It feels like I should be doing something, running, walking, but none of it matters. The train will get here when it gets here. The thing about Roman and Maurice is, they look like total schmucks, they play like schmucks. Worm is going to mark them the wrong way. This is important. But standing there on the platform, one of the thousand faces, I remember my briefcase sitting on the table still—that other life, that person I thought I was. It seems farther and farther away.

72

Jo will rescue it, I thought. Jo will rescue the briefcase and get me up to speed on moot court and drag my ass back on to the straight and narrow. Meanwhile I got to get to Worm before he manages to get himself hurt. Still I can see that briefcase sitting there on the table between the four of them and it's like it's zooming away from me, getting smaller and smaller. It's just the feeling in my head, I tell myself—no sleep the night before, not enough coffee or too much, it's hard to figure. Farther and farther . . .

The train comes and the usual zoom and rattle down thirty blocks. I can hear her voice: You lied to me. Another dead end. I keep running into them: the truck, Teddy's, now Jo . . . I have the feeling that I'm running out of time, I'm running, racing, and the clock is running out and I don't see a way out from where I am. It's just the lack of sleep, I tell myself, just the thirty-six hours and running on nerves. Still it's one of those truths where you find out and you know it's real, no matter how much you wish it wasn't: running out of time, running out of outs. What's next?

One foot in front of the other, I think: do what comes next, then see what happens. The train is hurtling forward through the darkness, carrying me with it, all these other anonymous faces. I'm not special. I'm just along for the ride. The random lights streak by between stations.

Up on the street again, the sunlight seems unreal, the passing people made of cardboard. Hurry, hurry, hurry, I think: and where does it get you? The daylight world, the shared hallucination. This is what I think sometimes: that it's just a big bowl of shit, except we all got together and agreed to call it ice cream. All this everyday, the work and the cars and the fancy fucking apartments. I only want it because the next guy wants it. Except I don't seem to want it anymore.

Up on the street: I'm the one who's racing through, dodging the other walkers. I am the asshole of the day for several pedestrians, or at least the first asshole of the day. I get to the Chesterfield at around eleven, early for some people, late for me and for Worm and for Petra.

She doesn't even say anything when she lets me in, just nods toward the table in the corner. And I can see that I'm too late: Roman and Maurice are already there, sitting at the table with the big-money black and gold checks in front of them and fucking Worm dealing.

"How long have they been here?" I ask her.

"Just an hour or so," she says.

"How come?" I ask her. "I never used to see these guys before noon."

"Roman's going away in the morning," she says. "What's the matter?"

"Nothing," I tell her, and drift over toward the table, trying to look like nothing, like smoke. It doesn't matter. They're hot on the showdown, I could land a 747 in there and they wouldn't notice. And here's the thing: in the Chesterfield, the same flat twenty-four-hour-a-day light and smoke, in the snap and rustle of the cards I feel at home. At least I know what's going on here. At least I know what the rules are.

I can see in Worm's eye that he's enjoying himself, and why not? He's got a nice big pile of other people's money on the table in front of him, and my guess is he's closing in on more. Here's what Amarillo Slim said: You can shear a sheep many times, but you can only skin him once—a lesson my pal Worm has never bothered to learn. He's already got these two stuffed and mounted over the fireplace and he's going back for more. If he thinks they're stewing now, wait till they find out how he beat them. It's a seven stud game, and he's got a pair of jacks sitting on his board.

Worm says, "Just the jacks . . ."

And Maurice shows two pair, tens and sixes. He's ready to take the pot. Then Worm turns his hole cards and shows a pair of sevens.

". . . and the sevens," he says.

"Motherfucker," Maurice says. "Slow rolling me like that. You said just jacks."

"Hey, hey," Worm says, and he's enjoying himself a little too much. It's these little flourishes that get him in trouble. "It's the cards that speak," he says. "I figured you read me for the sevens."

"Fuck," Maurice says, watching Worm rake the pot toward himself. He's already got a big stack there, too big a stack, I think, and much too quick. Maurice slams his fist onto the table, Roman tosses his hand into the muck like it was poisoned. It seems like about time to make an appearance, to distract them at least.

I step up into the light and grin at them. "Hey Roman, Maurice," I say.

"Mike," Roman says, glad for the break from losing. "You here to play? We need some new blood. They're putting the fucking bracelet on me tomorrow for four months, and I'm already stuck two racks."

"Well, have a good rest," I say, hoping this sounds okay to him. Then I turn to Worm: "Hey, cosmonaut, come here, get some air."

Roman stops for a second, looks from Worm's face to mine, trying to figure the connection. There's something about this he doesn't like. Worm himself looks sheepish, like I've come to take him to the principal's office. He organizes his checks in front of him, reluctant to leave them on the table. Because he cheats, he expects everybody else to. It comes to him like breathing.

"Leave it," I tell him. "It's fine."

He blinks at me, not quite understanding. But he follows me

anyway, gets up from the table and the Russians and follows me outside again.

Worm is stretching out in the daylight. He feels fine. He buys a bearclaw from a guy on the street and leans against the building, enjoying the sun.

"Where you at?" I ask him.

"Pumped up eight G's," he says. "I was ready to go on a run when you came along."

Asshole, I think. Eight thousand an hour is too much, much too much.

"All right," I tell him, buttonholing him against the building so I can keep my voice down. "Listen to me. You're in town five minutes, you already have a sign on your back."

I watch this news digest itself on his face, him figuring the angles until he finds one that works. Then the light goes on.

"That prick Knish," he says, throwing his bearclaw into the garbage. "Sees all the angles, never has the stones to play one."

Just like rain off a sidewalk, that's how deep my advice is going to get to Worm. The only question is whether he'll manage to get himself killed before he ends up back inside again. It's fucking depressing is what it is.

I tell him, "The guy hasn't had to work in fifteen years, Worm."

"What he does, grinding it out on his leather ass—that *is* work."

"I thought so, too," I tell him. "Now I know what work is. Speaking of which, why are you even playing at all? Don't you at least have to look for a job to stay out? Or are you just going to go back to printing those credit cards? Go away again?"

"I wasn't printing them," he says, looking caught again. "I was just distributing them."

That's it, I think: that's the thing that's missing in Worm, that voice inside him that says I should do that or I shouldn't do that.

For him it's all outside, it's what he can get away with and not get caught at. There's nothing inside him to slow him down.

"I'm never going back," he says, suddenly looking brighter. He's clean. "So what do you want me to do?"

"Think long term for once," I tell him. "Be smart. Everybody in here keeps books. You get listed as a mechanic, even if you don't get the shit beaten out of you, you won't be able to get action anywhere in New York. It's bad business."

You can see the calculations on his face, working the angles.

"Fucking Mikey," he says, still thinking. "Always seeing the big picture. . . . But you know what? I can't do what you do—bust games straight up, or work. This is how I live. You know me, I find a mark, I take him."

"I do know you," I tell him. "You're the guy who taught me how to play the angles. But right now you're the one with your nose open."

Rain off a sidewalk. He's getting away from me. I put my arm on his shoulder, just to keep him from giving me the slip.

"I'm not just preaching to you here," I tell him. "Those two aren't rabbits you're playing with. Roman and Maurice are Russian outfit guys."

This shows up on his face right away.

"Maybe not so bad as KGB," I tell him, "but nobody you want to fuck with either."

"Shit."

"It's not too late. You go in there and lose their fucking money back. You hear me? Nice and easy. Catch a run of real bad cards. Make it look good."

I'm losing him though. He thinks, he calculates. Then he looks up at me all pissed off, like I was his dad. Like I was a cop.

"Then what?" he says. "What do I do for money?"

"Take a trip to the suburbs," I tell him, and by then I'm practically begging him. "Find a nice dentist's game or something. Go back to Swan Meadows and play in that golf pro's game."

"Yeah, yeah, good idea, definitely," Worm says; and he's all outside again, all energy and talk. I've lost him. "Let me go in and do this. Meet me at Stromboli's, in about an hour."

"I can't," I tell him. "I've got a meeting and later I'm out to Queens to load the fucking truck."

"I see," Worm says; and in his eyes I can see that I'm the asshole now. He shrugs his shoulders, looks up and down the sidewalk—the usual collection of tics he develops when you're boring him, when you've disappeared already and he's waiting for you to go.

"Make it look good," I tell him, by way of good-bye. And Worm looks at me sincerely and he nods like a fucking altar boy at confession and then he's gone, back inside. Another dead end, I think. Another blind alley. It's too late for the rest of the meeting at the cafeteria, I know it. But the follow-up with Petrovsky isn't until four. I've got a couple of hours. Still I stand there, undecided: I could go *here*, I could go *there* . . . It's like it doesn't matter, like it's all the same. All this life around me, all this business and me stuck in the middle. Go home, the daylight voice says. Get some sleep. I know what I ought to do but I can't seem to do it.

Then I remind myself: One foot in front of the other, one thing at a time. Whatever is next. I start for home then, through the river of faces.

i sleep; and in my dreams I am on the train again, the uptown express, rocketing through the dark tunnel underground. Except this train doesn't stop, not at Times Square, not at One hundred twenty-fifth Street. It rocks and rumbles and shoots forward through the tunnel and I can't say for sure, but it feels like I'm the only passenger. I'm not looking around the car but out, at the lights trailing by—the random lights between stations, faster and faster. In the reflected window glass, though, the other seats are empty. And I remember the surprised look on the people in the stations when the train comes rocketing by so fast, the exact train they're waiting for and here it comes and it doesn't even stop! I can see their faces like in slow motion, in the instant that we pass: the expectation that the train is here, the train is come at last and then the slow realization that we are not going to stop, that this train is moving on, a hundred miles an hour. Looking back I can see them angry and jealous and I am the only one on this train, this is my train, I'm not going to stop for anything or anybody. . . . And then I hear the warning bell, the alarm, and I know we're coming to the end of the tracks, wherever that is, somewhere in Queens or Coney Island and I run up to the motorman's door and it's swinging open, empty. And the bell is ringing and the end of the tunnel is coming, I can't see it but I can feel it out there, the solid blank face of the rock wall in front of the train and we're not even slowing down and the bell is ringing and the train is rumbling.

And the bell is ringing and it's the telephone bell.

I wake up with my feet jammed through the bottom of the blankets, shivering with fear.

The telephone rings and rings again and then the answering machine picks up. When it's time for the message, I hear Jo's voice: "Mike? Mikey, are you there? Come on, pick up." A pause, she clears her throat, another pause. "I know you're there," she says, and gives this a minute to work. Then she says, "Fuck you, Michael."

I look at my watch and—shit!—it's five-thirty. I'm lying there drooling on the pillow while the Mulligan meeting is going, going, gone. Among other things, I think. Among other things. It takes me a minute to get going, though, all cobwebbed over with dreams, the train still beating along, the power of the thing and me along for the ride . . . I feel a little flutter of fear in my chest, not because of anything real.

I get up, pour a tray of ice cubes in the bathroom sink and fill it with water and then sink my face into it until I am clean of dreams, splashing the ice water on the back of my neck. I come up spluttering but I am awake now, and ready to go.

By the time I get to Jimmy Armstrong's bar, Jo is the only one left at the table, three or four empty chairs around it, a little forest of empty bottles and glasses in the center. It's been a jolly time. I hang back for a minute, watching her: she's beautiful, she's thinking. In a minute it's going to be arguments and noise and maybe tears but for now it's quiet. Potential energy, kinetic: everything's all wound up now, and it won't be pleasant or entertaining or sensible when it unwinds. I know I've gotten to her. I stand there at the edge of the crowd, out of her line of sight, and I try to think of some way to make it better. But it's just wishing. Dreaming. I've done things and I can't undo them. She's going to react.

Then I slide a chair out and sit down. She looks at me like she's seeing me for the first time; the way a stranger would look at you.

"Petrovsky waited and waited," she says, matter-of-fact. "So did the group."

"I looked all over for you," I tell her.

"You didn't want to be found."

"Jo, I missed one meeting—"

She loses patience with me here. This isn't what this is all about, we both know it, she isn't about to pretend along with me.

She says, "I don't care about the meeting. You know why I left this morning: I saw that gangster's roll in your pocket. That only means one thing with you."

"It's not what you think," I tell her—and it's not even a real lie, just a little light coating of bullshit, but it's enough to break her cool.

"Who am I, young Mary bimbo?" she yells at me. "You lie right to my face like this. Old days, you never lied. You lost everything, but at least you never lied."

She says it right to me, her eyes on me like a laser, right in her sights. But when she's done, she realizes that there are maybe fifty other people in this room, and that nearly all of them have stopped whatever they were doing before to watch the spectacle of us.

Jo tosses a twenty on the table and goes, out through the paralyzed crowd and onto the street. I walk out behind her, slow, feeling the eyes on me: the clean, functional, normal lives enjoying this. Fuck you and you and you, I think. Back to your TV and your talk. Leave me alone.

It takes me a minute to pick her up, out on the sidewalk, and another minute to come up even with her. I don't even know where she's going, and I bet she doesn't either—just out, out of the bar, away from me.

"Jo, look," I tell her. "It was hardly a real game. More like Wiffle ball."

She stops, middle of the sidewalk. Her cool is back.

"Funny," she says. "I can't remember the last time someone busted out playing Wiffle ball."

"The point is, I couldn't lose."

"No, Mike," she says, "You *can* lose." Then something changes; the hard shell melts for a second, and she's looking at me with something like tenderness. She's not even pissed anymore. This is worse. "Look, Mike," she says. "I watched you lose every dime you had, and I was still there. But I can't stay for this."

"Why does this still seem like gambling to you?" I ask her. "Why do you think the same five guys make it to the World Series of Poker every year? They're the luckiest guys in Vegas? It's a skill game, Jo."

"Then why'd you have to lie to me?"

Oh, Christ, I think: I'm feeling so many things that I can't even figure out what I'm feeling, pissed off at her—it's so fucking unfair of her—and at the same time I'm afraid of losing her and I know I'm losing her and it pisses me off and it isn't fair. What comes out is just whatever bubbles to the surface, and it happens to be the truth.

"This morning," I tell her, "I felt like shit for lying to you. But last night, when I sat down, I felt alive for the first time since I got broken at KGB's place. Can't you understand that?"

"Understand?" she says, lit up again. "Understand? You just said you felt alive for the first time sitting at a card table. What's that supposed to make me understand?"

Suddenly, it's like the picture where you look at it one way and you see a vase, another way it's two faces—I see that I've been saying the exact wrong thing, the exact thing that would push her away, while I'm trying to get her back with me again. And I've already said it and it's too late to unsay it and I am fucked.

"Look, what I meant—" I start, but she cuts me off.

"Do me a favor," she says.

"What?"

"Stay out of the apartment tonight, okay? Stay the hell away from me for a while. Go bother somebody else."

"What am I supposed to do?"

"That didn't seem to be a problem last night," she says. "You found your playmates all right. Look, just for tonight, okay? I mean, after you do your route, then maybe."

"I'm done with the route," I tell her. "I'm off the truck."

A little click. A little something in her face, a twitch, and then she's all outside again, all hard to the touch.

"I'll see you," she says, and reaches up, and touches my cheek, just once. And then she's down the sidewalk, gone.

here's a thing, I think in Superman, where it's Backwards Land, spelled Sdrawkcab. This is where everything works backwards: things fall up, clocks go from now till then, your shirt unbuttons down the back.

And how I ended up in Sdrawkcab, I couldn't tell you—except that here I am, somewhere in Brooklyn riding the train out to the end. Except that where I am is not nearly as important as where I am not: I am not at the Chesterfield, not out in Princeton, not riding the ten-twenty game at the goulash joint on Twenty-third, above all not at Teddy KGB's. I'm also not at home, not with Jo, not at work, not riding the truck, and not reading up for moot court. See? Backwards.

Also: the things I do to make my life better—working, studying—make me feel awful, while the things I do to screw my life up make me feel good. The things I say and do to get Jo back just seem to drive her away. The things I do to try and help Worm are likely to get him killed. It's better, I think, if I don't do anything at all. Then I think that if I don't do anything, that it's all going to come crashing down around me, that sudden collapse, that wreck at the end of the line. . . . And, you know, I like the feeling of being on the train, like the feeling of going somewhere and moving and so on and at the same time, I can't do anything real while I'm on it, anything to screw things up. But I can't help remembering the dream from this afternoon. I can't help being suspicious, that this might turn out to be the wrong thing.

That's it, I think: there's no right thing and no wrong thing. Or at least no way to tell them apart. I mean, I could go back, crawl into the apartment on my belly like a worm, maybe get Jo to take me back somehow. But riding the train, a hundred feet underground, I mean who's to say if that's the right thing or not? Maybe it's better for both of us if we're not together. Maybe it's better for her but not for me, or vice versa. It would be nice if there was some big neon sign over one of these alternatives: THIS IS THE RIGHT THING TO DO. What there is instead is the famous gray area. I seem to be stuck in the gray area.

I myself am longing for the green felt of the poker table, the simple world under the lights. At least there, I know what I want: I want to fuck you out of every last dime you've got, screw your women and drink your whiskey and steal your horses. It isn't complicated. Everybody else at the table wants the same thing. Somebody wins and somebody loses. From this distance, it seems so nice and clean.

Halfway to Coney Island I have made up my mind: Fuck it. Back to the city, back to the Chesterfield. Have some fucking fun for a change.

By the time we get to Coney Island, though, I am backwards

again: I've decided to get with the program, clean my skinny ass up and be like Michael Douglas, the suit, the hair.

Backwards, backwards, and backwards: by the time I make Manhattan again, I've definitely made up my mind in a half-dozen different directions. The only thing that sticks is this: I'm an ass-hole, any way you look at it. Also, I owe some apologies, starting with Petrovsky.

It's night when I make it back up on the street again, night and cold, ten-thirty or eleven. I know where he drinks—and he does drink—some horrible fake-English pub on Fifty-third I wandered into one night, looking for a place to make a phone call. I know where I ought to go but I don't want to go, but I make myself be-cause he was good to me. I owe him an explanation. Not that I exactly have an explanation. I'm fucked up is all.

I find him where he was before: a dark table in the corner, read-ing the newspaper, with a glass of gin at his hand and a bottle of gin on the table. I wonder how much of him is left, this time of the evening. He doesn't even notice me walking up, not till I pull the chair out across from him. When he looks up his face is a little thick, a little fuddled.

"Mind if I sit?" I ask him.

His eyes clear quickly, like clouds blowing out of a blue sky. As they clear, they take on a hard, unkind glitter.

"Well, Michael," he says. "That was a nifty trick the other night. At that point Marinacci and the D.A. were ready to cut cards for your services. Of course it was a different trick altogether, that disappearing act you pulled at your group's meeting today."

"That's why I'm here."

He doesn't soften. He takes a Pall Mall from his pack, Pat Nix-on's favorite cigarette, the alcoholic's choice, and he lights it and stares at me hard-eyed through the smoke. There is no kindness for me here, no mercy, no particular love.

"Your Jo, she's a good one," Petrovsky says. "She tried to cover for you. Kelly, on the other hand, was gunning hard to replace you as lead counsel."

"I guess I owe an explanation."

"Not to me," he says. "I'm sure there's a good reason you left. You'll have to work hard to prepare, and smooth things out with the others . . ."

He trails off, and as he does I watch his eyes cloud over again. He thought I was worth something; he was wrong; I'm free to go. I see that nothing I say or do is going to make a difference in this.

"All right then," I say, getting up to go. "I understand. Thanks for your time."

"Stay," he says, waving me down again. "Take a drink, Michael."

I recognize this reversal: the changeable weather of the alcoholic, the slippery shifts from a feeling to its opposite, the way his feeling can trap me inside it. Hi, Dad, I think. But this is only Petrovsky.

"What are you having?" I ask him.

"Gin," he says in a heavy, sad voice. "Always gin."

I take a glass off the next-door table and pour myself a drink, straight, no ice, no nothing. This is how Petrovsky takes it.

He says, "I know a magician's never supposed to tell his secrets, but let me ask you . . ."

"I'm no magician."

"So if it's not magic," he asks, "how did you know what they held?"

I can see the ex-prosecutor in him bearing down, searching for the guilty secret. He thinks I cheated my way into it. I make my explanation as clear and specific as I can.

"It's a combination of things," I tell him. "I watched as the cards came out. That's an old habit for me, like breathing. I saw Marinacci flinch when the three hit green."

"You watched the cards?" he asks.

"I watched the cards, also, but I watched the players reacting to the cards. I knew the D.A. made two pair the same way I knew Kaplan missed his flush, by following their eyes when they checked their river cards. Their faces told me everything."

"So you watch the man?" Petrovsky asks. He's getting excited, getting closer to the secret here. Something in him loves a con. Something in everybody but the judges most of all. He says, "I never thought I had to calculate so much at cards."

I've got him. I take one of his Pall Malls and stick it in my mouth.

"Most important thing," I tell him, "is premium hands. You only start with jacks or better split, nines or better wired, three high cards to a flush. If a bet's good enough to call, you're in there raising. Tight but aggressive. And I mean aggressive. That's your style, Professor. Always calculate. Think of it as war."

Petrovsky follows all this eagerly, letting the words sink in, trying to remember, to concentrate; but I see, at the end, that I have given myself away, too. He knows what I care about now. He knows what really matters to me; and again he has the upper hand.

"You are officially never invited to our game again," he says, smiling.

"I don't blame you," I tell him. I can't seem to stop. "You put a guy like me in a weak game like that, the cards themselves hardly matter. A fish acts strong, he's bluffing, acts meek, he has a hand."

But this is enough; he's getting tired of hearing about how bad a player he is. He flicks his cigarette in the ashtray and redirects.

"You know, Michael," he says. "It's the same in my vocation. In the courtroom, you'd be surprised how often it comes down to your ability to evaluate people."

My vocation, I notice. Not *our* vocation, but his. Something is being said here.

I tell him, "Of course you do have to know something about the law. I guess I should spend some more time studying *that*."

Petrovsky shrugs: maybe, maybe not.

"Let me tell you a story," he says. "For generations, the men of my family have been rabbis. In Israel and before that in Poland. It was to be my calling. I was quite a prodigy, Mike, the pride of my yeshiva. The elders said I had a forty-year-old's understanding of the midrash when I was twelve. By the time I was thirteen, though, I knew I could never be a rabbi."

"Why not?"

"Because for all I understood of the Talmud, I never saw God there."

He looks over at me, using his eyebrows to underline his words. He is talking to me. When he is satisfied that I understand the gravity of what he is saying, he goes back to his drink, and I think: Fuck you. He's just invited me to quit. I think: I don't need your drunk wisdom, your weight.

On the other hand: this is the only wisdom anybody has offered me lately.

"You couldn't lie to yourself," I say, making sure I understand him.

"I tried," he says, and grins—sourly, heavily. "Because I knew people were counting on me."

"But in the end, yours was a respectable choice."

"Not to my family," Petrovsky says. "My parents were destroyed by my decision. My father sent me away to New York to live with distant cousins . . ." He pauses, looking far away, some dime-store souvenir of Ellis Island, I think. The story and tragedy of Me.

Then returns to earth. He says, "Eventually I found my place, my life's work."

And I think: that's the difference between us; I could never say *my life's work* without cracking myself up. The story and tragedy of Me, I think, just the egotism of it. But then I think, maybe that's the thing that lets him be a great man, which he more or less is. Which I am not. Maybe I don't have it in me.

I ask him, "What happened then?"

"I immersed myself fully," he says. "I studied the minutia and learned everything I could about the law. I believed—I *believe*—it is what I was born to do."

"Your parents," I say. "Did they ever get over it?"

"No. They never understood how I consorted with criminals, how I defended murderers, rapists, thieves. They considered what I did dishonorable. I always hoped I might do something to change their minds, but they were inconsolable. My father wouldn't speak to me."

And this is why he is speaking to me; the message is unspoken, unmistakable.

"They died before I became a teacher," he says.

Here is the choice, I think. This is what he is offering me: the freedom to go either way, to take either branch. And I am enough of an asshole to resent him for it: who is he to judge me? What gives him or anybody the right? But what he's offering me is real, I think, and worth something, and so I should just shut up. Pay him his piece of silver, his tribute, and accept his gift.

I ask him, "You'd still make the same choices?"

"What choice, Michael?" He sits up, and his eyes have the same hard glitter in them that they had when I first sat down. "What choice?" he says. "The last thing I took from the yeshiva is this: We can't run from who we are. Our destiny chooses *us*."

He holds my eyes with his and I see the rabbi in him, the rabbi he has become despite himself: friendly, stern, correct. The steel backbone, underneath. He is right and he knows it and if I don't agree, it's pride and nothing else. Pride and sin. After a minute he looks away, takes a sip of gin, and laughs.

"Fancy words," he says, and laughs again. "Destiny, huh?"

"No, I appreciate it."

"You can only care about what you care about," he says, lighting a fresh Pall Mall from the butt of the old one. "That's all."

"Well, thanks."

"Thanks for keeping me company," he says, drawing the newspaper toward him off the table. "I will see you in moot court? Yes?"

"I'll be there," I tell him.

He looks at me, still questioning. But my audience is over. On my way out of the bar, I look back and Petrovsky is sitting exactly as he was when I came in, reading the same page of the same newspaper, holding the same glass of gin. The table is brown, the wall behind him is brown, the light is yellow with cigarette smoke. He looks ageless, demonic. I wonder if he sleeps at all.

A moon between the buildings, out on the street.

I drift along with the others, the faces, the ebb and flow of traffic, talkers, walkers, men with missions. I'm going: where? I ought to be up in the Bronx right now, loading Knish's truck, but I don't seem to be. He's got a backup, he'll be fine. Nobody will miss their Ding-Dongs in the morning. You can only care about what you care about: I can't figure out whether Petrovsky meant this as a blessing or as a curse.

It's late, near midnight. I told Jo I'd stay out of her way but I'm in my constructive mode: get everything out of the way, apologies, arguments, all the human shit. And then what? Something, I think, something new.

So I drift back toward the apartment, knowing I lied to her, knowing she busted me on it. It's a fact I would just as soon forget. It wasn't exactly a lie, not when I was telling it, but when she found the roll it turned into one in a second, and now we've got to figure some way to work it into the general story, the Story of Us. Who we are and what we are like. Now one of us is a liar. This is going to be difficult.

So I am not best pleased when I round the corner and Worm is standing on my doorstep. It's a cold night and it looks like he's been there a while.

"Hey, kemosabe," he calls out, clutching his jacket around him. It's cold, damp.

When I get up into the light, I see that somebody has been working him over. His face is beaten and bloody, one corner of his mouth swollen up like a pair of candy lips, and he stands slightly doubled over around his belly. Somebody has been hitting on Worm, hitting hard.

"What the hell happened to you?" I ask him.

"I cut myself shaving," he says. "Ran into a door. What do you want to know?"

It's a good question. I don't really want to know. At this point, I don't want to be carrying any more of Worm's shit around—I've got enough of my own, and besides, all my help doesn't seem to help him. I don't really want to know who beat him up, or why. I'll find out eventually, when he wants something from me.

"Can I come in?" he asks.

Fucking great. His timing is perfect. But I can't say no.

"Sure," I tell him. "Of course. Just tone it down, though, please. Things haven't been that smooth on the homefront."

"Tone what down, motherfucker?"

"Forget it," I tell him, looking at his grin in the lobby light. And I tell you what: the little bastard does cheer me up. I've got a little voice like that in my head, too. No, you fuck you. The thing with Worm, he hasn't got any other voices, just the one. We walk up the four flights to the apartment, and he's breathing hard at the top.

Inside, I turn on the lights and the couch is gone, the dining room set, the end tables and lamps. I understand right away: she's cleared out.

"What the fuck?" Worm says, looking around at the bare floors and walls. "You been robbed?"

"Not exactly."

"I see the combinations working on his face, sorting through the possibilities until he comes up with the answer.

"She's gone, huh?" he asks.

I don't say anything, just walk through the rooms, looking at the places where her stuff used to be. There isn't much left. I wonder what part of me was expecting this. It's not even that she's gone— it's just the timing, the way she did it so soon. Just the logistics of getting a fucking couch moved in this city. She's a capable girl.

"You don't seem surprised," Worm says.

I shake my head. "You won't find any note," I tell him. "She's not the type to leave one. I always told her she'd be a good player."

Worm angles his head toward me, curious as to what I mean.

"She'd know when to release a hand," I tell him. "The minute it couldn't be won."

"Smart girl," Worm says.

"Oh, yeah," I tell him, and keep on circling the apartment. I can't make myself sit still. I seem to need the evidence: the blank places on the walls, the dents in the carpet where the chairs used to be. And Worm is there to see it and I'm the asshole in the case. I'm the one who got left, who got dumped—though if I was Jo, I know I could argue it the other way. What was her choice?

"Damn it," I say, just to the room at large. "I knew I couldn't bluff her."

"Bluff her?" Worm says. "Shit, man, you can never trust 'em. Look at you—you domesticate yourself, take yourself out of the life, you walk the fucking line. You sacrifice for men, and then she's gone. It's like the saying goes: If life is a poker game, then women are the rake, man. Women are the fucking rake."

"What saying is that?"

"I don't know man, there ought to be one."

He looks down at me, expecting the laugh, but I don't feel like laughing. Worm lights a cigarette and thinks through the smoke. He never runs out of ideas, though he sometimes runs out of good ideas.

He asks me, "You know what always cheers me up when I'm feeling shitty?"

"What's that?"

"Rolled up aces over kings."

"Is that right?"

"Check-raising stupid tourists, and taking fat pots off of them calling stations."

"Yeah?"

"Stacks and towers of checks," Worm says. "High-stakes Hold 'Em all night at the Taj . . ."

He gets this dreamy look, thinking of all the fish of Atlantic City, the money just waiting for him. And he's beat-up outside and I'm beat-up inside and there isn't anything much for me here: a night in an empty apartment, a laundry list of all the things I could have or should have. . . . And then all those fish, those human get-well cards wandering the boardwalk with their wallets full. I'm ready to dump a little of this shit on somebody else for a change, I think. I'm ready to reach out.

"Fuck it," I tell Worm. "Let's go."

"Serious?" he says, surprised.

"Serious, yeah. Let's do it."

"Now we're talking," he says, suddenly alive; and for the moment we're both sixteen again, full of piss and plans, ready to go. The world opens up again, fresh and full of possibility, a nice big blank slate for us to write our names in. This is what I was missing, I think. This is what I was after.

We rent a car—I know there are places where you can't rent a car at quarter to midnight, and I do feel sorry for the people who live in them—we rent a car and take off down the turnpike before the good feeling can wear off. I've still got the keys to the Cherokee and I think for a minute that we could take it. But that's one step farther than I need to go tonight. A trip out of town, a few bright lights, a little money in my pocket—that's all I need for tonight. We drive down quietly, me hanging with the thought of Jo, Worm thinking about whoever it was that beat him up. I'm still waiting for the story.

Now, the poker room at the Mirage in Vegas is the center of the poker universe. Doyle Brunson, Johnny Chan, Phil Helmuth—the legends—consider it their office. Every couple of days a new millionaire shows up wanting to beat a world champion. Usually they go home with nothing but a story.

Here in Atlantic City, though, the millionaires are scarce, or else they're playing craps. But there's still plenty of money for the taking. In fact, on the weekends you can't get a game in the city, because all the New York rounders are taking care of the tourists down here. We roll in about one-thirty, prime time, head straight for the Taj and dump the car, and the morning spreads out fresh and sweet in front of us as we walk in under the lights.

"You know what?" Worm says as we walk in. "You play. I'm going to attend to certain other needs."

"Good," I tell him. "I was starting to get worried about you. I thought maybe the boys upstate brought about some changes."

"In your dreams, lover boy," he says, and heads off for the bar. He won't have any problem getting what he wants in there, assuming that's where he's going and what he wants. You never know with Worm. There's always something left out, a side to the story you don't know.

Myself, I head for the poker room: an airplane hangar decorated in gilt and whorehouse velvet, three big screens of horse races along the back wall, the sweat and smoke of seventy-five tables going all at once, filling the room with noise. The pit bosses race around in shiny suits, calling empty seats into their walkie-talkies, filling the places with conventioneers from the floor. Tonight is polyester night, as always, with a scattering of natural fibers from the teachers' convention in town. Cotton, wool, naturally graying hair—what Jo used to call the Connecticut look—looks about as at home on the floor here as a sponge-diver's suit would. This is the natural habitat of plastic.

Halfway back through the room I find a nest of familiar faces: Zagosh, Savino, Petra, a couple of others. There's a seat open at the table, waiting for me. I take out five hundred of the college boys' money and slip it to the dealer as I'm taking my place.

"Changing five hundred," the dealer says as she gives me my checks. "Good luck, sir."

The faces look up, familiar, bored.

"Beautiful," I tell them. "Welcome to the Chesterfield South. I come all the way to Atlantic City just to look at you mugs."

"Nice to see you, too, asshole," Savino says.

"Twice in one week," Petra says. "For someone who doesn't play, you spend a lot of time in card rooms."

Christ, is she available. Come to think of it, so am I. But first we have cards to play.

"Ten-twenty Hold 'Em," the dealer announces, starting the ritual. "Pay your time."

We each put up a couple of checks—the casino's money—and then the pit boss brings over a plastic bag with a couple of fresh decks in it and we wait while the dealer makes the new decks. And here I am: back again. I feel the ease and expectancy of the night ahead, the green felt under the big light. This, this right here, is the one place I know what I'm doing. The blinds go up and the cards come down and after that I'm fine, the game takes over, nothing but the game, none of the extra shit.

A hand or two passes—nothing much is going to happen here, not between these pros—when I spot Joey Knish coming out of the crowd. We're on the turn, and Freddy Face has called time. Joey walks up behind me and puts his hands on my shoulders, just like he owns me.

"This is what I like to see," he says. "Michael McDermott where he belongs, sitting with the scumbags, dragging the occasional pot."

"Occasional?" Freddy Face says. "Like my ex-wife *occasionally* went out with other men. I call."

"Forget her, Face," says Joey. "Now, I was going to actually try and make some real money tonight, but in honor of Mike's Ali-like return to the ring, I'll sit with you all for a while."

"Don't do us any favors," Petra says. "They're about to go to the board to fill these seats. I raise."

Knish sits down anyway. Zagosh looks from him to Petra and back, trying to figure out who he's most annoyed with.

He says, "If we wanted to try and take each other's rolls, we could have stayed back home. I fold."

"Fold," says Freddy Face, and the dealer pushes the pot toward Petra, who manages to look extremely bored.

Before the next hand is dealt, a floorman comes by, sees the empty seats, and sticks his hand in the air, two seats. In a minute we get the fish: a pair of conventioneers, out on a lark. Middle-aged men, they look okay in their suits, they look like they're comfortable telling other people what to do. These two have *no fucking idea* what they're about to walk into. Each of them drops a few hundred on the table, figuring, why not give it a try? How different can it be from the game on the corner?

"Five hundred," the dealer says, trading their cash for checks. "Good luck, gentlemen."

Luck, I think. All the luck in the world isn't going to change things for these guys. They're simply overmatched. Everybody wants to believe in luck, like it's the magic dust, you never know where it's going to fall. But those same ten guys make it back into the World Series every year. They don't have any lucky dust. They know how to play the game is all, better than anybody else.

So: Claude and Jason and their magic lucky dust sit down at the table, and we chew on them for a while, and then we take them down. We're not exactly playing together, but we're not playing against each other, either. It's like the Nature Channel: you don't see piranhas eating one another, now, do you? We quit acting like we know each other, we settle down to business while Claude and Jason drink and bluff and make bad bets. I mean, maybe these guys know how to sell lawnmowers or whatever the fuck they do. But they can't even play their own hands, much less figure any of the rest of us out. They get hands that I'd win with and run them into the ground. By the time they're gone—about forty-five minutes—I'm sick of both of them. It's like one of those fucking Vietnam movies where you spend the first half hour getting to know the platoon and the rest of the movie watching them die painful deaths. You can see it coming, they can't. It's not that much fun.

So: so long Claude and Jason, hello Mark and Angela. They're on their honeymoon!

So long, Mark and Angela! Hello Larry and David!

We rotate them through at hour-long intervals, more or less, depending on the size of the roll and the amount of magic fairy dust they carry with them. The more luck they have, the better for us: they stay in longer, pry the wallet from the pocket, and buy in deeper, waiting for the lucky dust to come back to them. They're all still waiting. And Worm was right, it does no doubt cheer me up. Just the sight of all those nice fresh chips on the table in front of me cheers the hell out of me. And look, I'll tell you, I'm sure this doesn't do me any credit in anybody's eyes, but I do love that hurt look on their faces, on their way out. These dumbass motherfuckers come onto my ground and try to play my game with me and think they can get away with it. It's only justice when they lose. It does make me happy, yes it does.

Time passes, the river of cards and bets and bluffs and checks. They don't keep clocks in here and they don't have windows. And none of us—none of the regulars, I mean—keep watches, or at least we don't wear them. Time comes down to this: Are you making mistakes yet? Is there money on the table? If there's money to be made, and you're awake enough to take it, then it isn't bedtime yet. After that, it's just numbers on a dial.

So I don't know how much later it is when Worm comes into the room and finds me. He comes in between fish, and sits down in one of the open seats next to Knish, to the general annoyance of everybody. Plus there's that little shock from his face, which is still beat-up, swollen. He reaches across Knish and grabs a stack of my chips and sets them in front of himself on the table.

"Good," Knish says to me. "That's the way to build the bankroll back up."

"Sir?" the dealer says to Worm, but he's listening to Savino.

"Worm, good to see you," says Savino. "Glad you're out. Number's changed, of course, new number. A lot of games this weekend, so if you're going to call and put down some action, you're going to need the new number."

"Worm, let me ask you," says Zagosh, a little less friendly. "Are you allowed in places like this?"

Worm says, "What are you, my fucking P.O. now, Zagosh? I didn't think you had a job."

"Sir?" the dealer says again. "I'm sorry, sir, you can't take chips from another player at the table."

Worm looks around, like he was waking up from a dream. He recognizes all the faces.

"It's all right, honey," he explains to the dealer. "We're all friends here."

"I'm sorry, sir, you'll have to buy your chips from me."

Worm looks from her to the table to the other faces, disgusted.

He puts the checks back. He goes to his pocket but all he comes up with is a voucher.

"Fuck it," Worm says. "Mike, let's hit the noodle bar. I got us comped."

"I could have some soup," I tell him. Time for a break anyway.

Knish says, "Oh, look who's treating us to a free meal. Don't let that MSG fuck up your head any more than it already is, Mikey."

I wave him off, leave my checks at the table, follow Worm through the hum and smoke and sweat of the card room, through the lobby and under the red-and-gold arch of the Dragon Room. In the red darkness inside are tables and tables of Chinese and Vietnamese, all men, all smoking, all playing their incomprehensible games, waving cards in the air, shouting in Cantonese. The noodle bar is in the corner, one little counter and an antique chef who looks like he was carved from Chinese wood, a long time ago. We point our way through the menu and he nods. He looks like he's ready to kill us.

"What the fuck are you sitting in that rock garden for?" Worm asks. "You can't get paid in a game that tight. Get serious here."

"I like playing with these guys."

"These guys have no ambition," Worm says. "They're content to sit around ten-twenty splitting two slobs' money five ways. What we need to do is move up to fifty-hundred, find some rich suckers. A table full of them."

"I'm not playing short-stacked in a game like that," I tell him. "I'll walk out of here with a grand, easy, tonight."

"A grand," Worm says, like he was spitting on it. "Happy to make a grand. After driving three fucking hours to get here."

This is starting to piss me off. If I need a lecture at all, it isn't from Worm, not from a guy with nothing in his pockets and a lip like Betty Boop.

I tell him, "Any time I get up with more than I sat down with, it's a good day on the job."

"The job?" Worm says. "The *job*? Now you're starting to sound like that sanctimonious prick, Knish."

"Why don't you calm down?" I ask him.

"Oh, I'm calm," he mutters, darkly. "Real calm." He sees I'm serious and he gets that sailor's leer on his face. Loudly, grinning, he says, "You should have seen this little skirt I just twirled."

When he's sure that everybody's watching him, he makes a circle of his thumb and forefinger and starts to pump his finger though, making loud sucking noises. It's either laugh with him or kill him; so I laugh.

"You know something?" I ask him. "You're all elegance and grace, Worm."

He doesn't say anything, just rubs the side of his nose with his upraised middle finger, just like back in the sixth grade. The antique cook comes up to the counter then with two bathtubs of noodle soup, looking secretly pleased, like he had just spit in them.

"Pass the hot sauce," Worm says.

DELICIOUS HOT CHILI GARLIC SAUCE, it says on the side of the label, with a rooster breathing its last on the label. I take a whiff in passing: red-chili rocket fuel.

"Careful with that shit," I tell Worm. "It'll burn a hole right through your stomach."

Worm nods vigorously at me, then spoons two big doses into his soup and stirs it in, turning the whole bowl an evil diluted-blood pink color. Another strikeout for common sense.

"So Mr. Nick the Greek," I ask him, "how come you're kiting my chips instead of helping your own cause?"

"I'm on empty, that's why."

"Tapped out again? How much was that hooker, anyway?"

"Please, Mike, relaxation therapist," he says, cracks up on his own joke, then takes a long slurp out of his bowl. But then his face tightens up. He says, "But that's not where it went."

He waits for me to figure it.

"Roman and Maurice?" I ask him. "I told you to give back but come on. You could have kept something for your time."

"That's not where it went, either," he says; picks up his bowl and drinks the last of the broth from it, sets it down, wipes his lips with a napkin. The story is coming, he won't be hurried. The story is all he's got. Finally he says, "Ran into fucking Grama today."

"Yeah?"

"He wasn't seeking re-employment."

Grama is this pimp that used to work for Worm sometimes. I mean, he's literally a pimp, but that's also the nicest thing you could say about him. Grama is about the lowest rung of dimwit street muscle you can imagine.

"Who does he work for then?" I ask him.

"He's, uh, he's on his own now," Worm says, looking sincere, which means he's lying. Why would he lie about this? But I'm going to have to wait until all the little jigsaw pieces of the story come out before I can try and fit them together.

"He's buying up debt," Worm says. "He relieved me of all my holdings."

"Took your whole roll off you," I say, and Worm nods grimly. "That cocksucker. Turncoat bastard. So now you owe *him* the ten."

Worm looks away, just a degree away from my eyes, like he's ashamed of himself.

"Not by his math," he says.

"How fucking much, Worm?"

A little flash of anger in his eyes, a little flash of fear.

"He says I owed fifteen," Worm says. It costs him to get it out, his lips twisted up funny. "With the juice, I guess it's near double that now."

He goes back to his empty soup bowl, leaving me to react to the number. If this actually is the number; I wouldn't put it past Worm to drop a couple thousand off the total. He's not compulsively addicted to the truth. But even if it's only twenty-five, it's still bad. Worm has never once been anywhere close to that far ahead, not once in his life. And Grama is definitely dumb enough to be dangerous.

"That's where the facial work came from?" I ask him.

Worm rubs the side of his face where it's still swollen and nods. "He fucking tracked me down in Billy's Topless," he says. "I was just sitting there watching the dancers, minding my own business. Completely uncalled for."

But this is just posture, posture and positioning. I see that Worm really doesn't give a shit about taking care of himself, I see it and it pisses me off. Makes me feel like the sucker, trying to keep him alive.

"Why didn't you tell me it was that bad?" I ask him. "Let me pay toward it when I could have."

"It's my problem," he says. "Jesus Christ, I'm going to have you pay what I owe? I'll have you help me, like we used to. It's why we're here. But I'm no leech."

"All right, all right," I tell him. I hate it when Worm starts talking about his principles. "Of course I'll help. I am helping. But Grama, shit."

We sit there a minute or two, aimed off in different directions. He's said his piece, handed me his trouble. Now I've got to figure

out what to do with it. I'm trying to concentrate but I keep thinking about Jo. Specifically I'm wondering about the couch and the
rest of the big shit. I mean, she could get her clothes out in an
evening, the books she needed. But she had to get the movers in,
find a place to put the stuff, she's sleeping someplace tonight.
She's got this other place, out in the world somewhere; and I'm
here trying to figure out how to take care of Worm, same as always,
same as the sixth grade. It occurs to me, not for the first time, that
she was right about me.

"Maybe we can talk to Grama," I say to Worm. "Get you some
time off the vig."

Worm looks at me like I just fell off the turnip truck.

"I doubt it," he says. "You don't know how he feels about me,
man. I wasn't the most understanding boss."

"Fuck him," I say, and pat Worm on the back, just to let him
know I'm on the case. "We'll figure something out. I got to get back
to the table."

He looks up at me, grateful, then grins it all away.

"Hey, man," he says. "Could you leave a tip?"

no windows, no clocks, no watches. I'm up about thirty-two hundred dollars on the night and feeling fine, good to go, and then: a horrible thought occurs to me.

"Petra," I say. "What day is it? Do you know?"

"I think it's Tuesday, Mike. How come?"

"Fuck," I tell her. "Fuck!"

"What?"

"Moot court," I tell her, gathering my checks in a hurry. "I don't have time to explain. Anybody seen Worm?"

They all look at me like I've lost my mind, all but the three late-nighters who are feeding the table. They look from face to face, realizing for the first time that we might know each other. That look I love comes on their faces, the slow dawning of awareness, that sudden realization of their place in the food chain. You're prey, baby! But I don't have time to really enjoy it, don't have time to find Worm, don't have time to do much of anything except cash out at the cashier's window and ransom the rent-a-car. If Petra's right, moot court starts in three hours and twenty minutes and I am fucked.

It's just light, cold and damp, as I head out of Atlantic City, driving exactly seven miles over the speed limit. A ticket would cost me more time than I could ever gain from going fast, and New Jersey, in my experience, is lousy with cops. Asshole, asshole, asshole, I think—it's a word I come back to again and again. One last chance to prove yourself to Jo and you fucked it up, asshole. You left Worm stranded in Jersey, asshole. That hole card you got yourself with Marinacci and this is your only chance to play it, asshole—and so on, with variation and repetition. The traffic clots and slows as we get closer to the city, the worker bees heading for their places. I can feel the one big vein on the side of my forehead starting to swell up, driving along at twelve miles an hour. In my head, I rehearse the case and how I will present it, if I get a chance to: one step at a time, this then this then this: Good morning, Judge Marinacci. . . . In my head, I rehearse the small movements that will maybe, *maybe*, get me to the court on time: where my briefcase is, my suit, which necktie . . .

I am exactly twenty-two minutes late when I make it into the courtroom.

The good news is, they haven't started yet. This is the bad news, too—I've succeeded in wasting the time of everybody else in the courtroom, and they're all pretty pleased about it, especially the judges. It's Marinacci—no more Gene for me, I think—Petrovsky, and McKinnon, a black man with a stare like a wounded eagle. The judges are judging on me, hard.

"Perhaps we can begin now?" says Petrovsky.

"Sorry I'm late," I tell him, the lamest thing ever spoken by man, it feels like. I set my guilty little briefcase on the table and rummage desperately through for my papers, feeling the eyes of the room on me. There's some kind of horrible sweat rising out of the inside of my suit jacket and I'm trying to remember where I wore it to last.

"You ready?" Jo asks.

I don't know what she's trying to say with this, and when I look into her face there's nothing for me; a poker player's blank.

Marinacci begins while I'm fumbling the papers out. He says, "Come to order in the matter of Slater versus New York State Higher Education Services. The facts have been stipulated, the briefs have been read. Lead counsel for the plaintiff, Mr. McDermott, please proceed with oral arguments now. If that's convenient for you."

I was feeling better right up till that last sentence—all the high-flown legal rhetoric carrying me along, making me feel a part of something—but now I realize: they're not here to help me. They don't give a shit if I fail. It's a moment, like in a game, when you're bluffing and you know you've been found out and there's no choice, you've got to keep up the bluff. You watch your money go, bet by bet, raise by raise.

"Yes sir, Your Honor," I tell him. Zipping right along. I still can't find the right folder but I can do it from memory, maybe. "Clearly," I say, "the case that controls the issue at bar is Texas versus Johnson, which holds . . . which holds . . ."

"Texas versus Johnson?" Marinacci says. "Mr. McDermott, that is a Supreme Court free speech case that has no bearing here. Each group was apprised to ignore that aspect of this matter and focus instead on the idea of de facto segregation."

A silence in the courtroom. I have fucked the dog and every-

body knows it, everybody sees. I look from face to face and every-
body looks away, everybody but the judges, who are busy judging.
I'm poisoned with the same deep failure as that night at Teddy
KGB's. Nobody wants to catch it from me.

Then Kelly, plucky Catholic schoolgirl, steps up to save the day.
"Mr. McDermott has been unreachable," she says. "I'll take over
now, if that pleases the court.

Marinacci says, "Somebody saying something meaningful
would please us a great deal."

Before Kelly can start, he gives Petrovsky a look—from his face
to mine and back again—and I see Petrovsky shrug and shake his
head, ever so gently. More in sorrow than in anger. Fuck you and
you and you, I think. Fuck all of you. It's just like that night at
KGB's except for two things. First: once my part is over, once I
have fucked the dog, I still have to sit there and sit there and sit
there while the case is argued and counterargued and rebutted
and so on by every other joker in the room. No stepping out in the
alley with Knish to smoke a joint, no matter how much I wish I
could.

The other thing: I realize, as I sit there listening to them argue it
out, that I'm really not that worried about it. Yes, it's two years of
my life, almost three. Yes, indeed, I did drive that fucking truck
all winter to keep this thing going. And yes: if I could only care
enough, if I could only pretend to care enough, I'm smart enough
to do this. I could run rings around Kelly. I could wear a suit and
marry Jo and make friends with the nice furniture. But I can't.

I can only care about what I care about. I look up at Petrovsky
and he won't give me his eyes. I'm ashamed of letting him down
this way but the thing is, he knew. He knew. So did Jo. I suspect I
was wearing this on my face a long time before I ever figured it
out myself. And Jo: she's keeping busy, keeping her eyes off me,

organizing the notes and feeding them to Kelly. Question: Is it her? or is it the dream of a better life, the Connecticut hair and cheekbones, the Michael Douglas dream. . . . It doesn't matter, she's gone anyway. But looking at her, watching her work, I think that she understands me. I think of her on the bed, half-naked, drinking wine at three in the morning and counting up the money, and I know she could do this with me. It''s like she's cut herself off, not just from me but from all the longings, all the things that don't fit with the lawyer thing. And I feel sorry for her, and I want to bring her with me, wherever the hell I'm going . . .

The minutes crawl by like crippled ants, one by one. The smell rises off the inside of my jacket: sweat and aftershave and something else. Did I loan it to somebody? Is this jacket even mine?

Then, somehow, it's over. Words are being spoken, the other team is slapping each other on the back, hearty on victory. Although the verdict won't come in till next week, and although Kelly has done a wonderful job of trying to cover for me, we all know that we lost. Also, that it's all my fault.

Griggs whacks me on the back as soon as we get out of the courtroom.

"That was impressive!" he says. "Usually you know what the case is about when you give an opening statement."

"I was a little less prepared than I thought . . ." I tell him. Really, I don't care.

"It worked out great for me," Kelly says brightly. "I think I actually impressed Marinacci."

Fuck you, I think. You and you and me, too. Everybody but Jo. I pull her aside and the others pass on. She doesn't exactly look like she wants to.

"We need to talk about this," I tell her. "You moved pretty fast on me."

"You make it sound like it was my decision."

"It wasn't mine," I tell her. "I come home and you're gone."

I look at her face, trying to read into her eyes, but there's nothing there for me. I know she loves me, I know she belongs with me. I know if I could find the right words, I could make her see that. I also know that there aren't any magic words.

"How could you give up on me so quick?" I ask her, sounding exactly like the fucking loser I am. That's the way to win her back, I tell myself: sound as pathetic as possible. Chicks dig a pathetic guy.

"I learned it from you, Mike," she says. "You always told me this was the rule, rule number one: throw away your cards the minute you know you can't win. 'Fold the fucking hand.' That's a quote, Mike."

"This is *us* we're talking about," I tell her—I whine, actually, I can hear it. "This isn't some losing hand of cards."

"I know what we're talking about," she says. And suddenly she's neat, sharp, buttoned-up again. The little opening I saw in her eyes is closed again, leaving a brittle hard shell, her on the inside, me on the outside.

"So this is the last of it," I say.

"That's right," she says. "This is where I get off."

"Jo," I say to her. Then I run out of words.

Then comes one of these silences where she's waiting for me to say something and I'm running the combinations in my head, looking for the right thing, and there's nothing there and she's going to make this mistake, yes she is. And I think about that sweetness. I think about my dick inside her, the way our bodies fit together, moved together, and I know that's over and done with. And there's nothing I can say, nothing I can do. But she's waiting.

"You're overreacting," I finally tell her—which is *exactly* wrong, it pisses her off, I can see it in her eyes. I've got a talent. But I can't seem to stop myself. "It's not like I'm out running around on you," I tell her. "Look, I want to make things right."

"You know," she says, "most of my friends wonder, at least sometimes, if their husbands or boyfriends cheat on them. I never had to worry about that. It was never some chick, it was always Worm. The only other woman was poker."

"Look . . ." I start out. "Babe . . ."

But this is her moment, her exit line, the one she's been practicing.

"I'd say good luck, Mike," she says. "But I know it's not about luck in your game. See you."

Turns, and walks away, and leaves me standing there looking after her. Another dead end, I think. Another blind alley. I'm starting to wonder if there's one to lead me out of here.

day sleeping. I wake up on a pillow damp with my own drool, with the memory of a dream just out of reach. Something about a meadow, something about horses and women. Then I was a soldier. Something bad happened, I can't quite put my finger on it.

It's five-thirty. Dirty daylight sneaks through the curtains, into the apartment but not quite into the corners. I can feel my motor starting up, the usual sense of urgency—got to get going, don't get too far behind, got to keep moving—but then I remember that I've got no particular place to go. I'm not driving the truck anymore. I'm sure not going to waste any more of my time in the law library. Nobody's waiting for me, nobody's looking for me, nobody's counting on me, assuming Worm did find a ride back from Atlantic City. It's a strange feeling for me: lying in bed an extra minute, trying to relax.

I'm not built for it though. It only makes me nervous. Maybe if I still smoked, I could handle it—I remember high school, hanging around for hours doing nothing but smoking cigarettes—but I don't light them anymore. Though, if you take the long view, there's not much point in that anymore, either. It's my life. I don't owe anybody anything. I ask myself the ex-smoker's question: have things gotten legitimately bad enough to let me smoke again?

Not quite, I think, going over the list: war, clinical depression, terminal illness. Getting dumped did not quite qualify. Still it seems a little silly to save up anything for the future. I don't have a future anymore, at least not one I can imagine. Jo is out, the law is out, the Michael Douglas thing with the suits and the cars. And every time I think about playing, all I can remember is the smile on Teddy KGB's face at that last showdown. I mean, yeah, I can beat office-supply salesmen and convention-goers in Atlantic City all I want. But, you know, a second-rate rounder. . . . Somehow I made it all the way from my childhood to here and now here I am, stuck.

I get up, get moving, make some coffee. I take a count of what's left, now that Jo has cleared out: the kitchen table and chairs, mismatched kitchen junk, a mattress, a TV and VCR, and a hundred books about poker. I drink my coffee and read S&M—in this case Sklansky and Malmuth, who wrote the book on Hold 'Em. I remember the excitement when I first read it; I remember studying it like it was the Bible, like Petrovsky memorizing the holy secrets. So much energy, so much faith tied up in that dream. But now, at the end of that alley, there's only the smiling face of KGB, the knowledge—the certainty—that in the end I am not one of the winners.

Petrovsky, though: I owe him an apology.

Take care of business, I think. Then figure out what's next. The apartment, for instance, is still a wreck. I've got two years of law-school notes to toss in the basement, several souvenir pictures of me and Jo that I know I'll regret tossing sometime later but they've got to go. Keep moving, I think, and maybe sometime, somehow, you'll figure out why you're moving and where you're trying to get to. Or maybe not.

The apartment is as tidy as it's going to get by nine o'clock, the night just starting and me all turned around, day for night. I want that last appointment with Petrovsky. I owe him. But I can't quite bring myself to leave the apartment, I don't want to see that look of disappointment in his eyes. The weight of his judgment. By the time I get uptown it's late, by his standards anyway, quarter to eleven. I see the empty chair in the corner of the pub, as soon as I walk in.

"Have you seen Abe Petrovsky?" I ask the bartender.

"Almost every day I've worked here," he says, grinning like he's making a joke. "Already been and gone tonight though. Can I get you something?"

"Gin," I say, in Petrovsky's honor. "I'll have a gin."

But sitting on a barstool in an empty bar doesn't calm me down any. I've still got that restlessness. I think about the Chesterfield, a few blocks across town: the regular faces, the certainty of that green-felt place under the lights. I could sit down now and not get up till Friday. I've still got the cash from Atlantic City in my pocket.

I don't want to though.

This is weird, it's like not wanting to have sex or something. But I just have this feeling—I want to get clear about things, what I want and where I'm going. Otherwise I'm just drifting, going with the current, a piece of trash bobbing along. A night at the Chesterfield turns into a week which turns into a year and then I wake up some morning and I'm Knish, fifty years old. It's not that I don't like Knish. I just don't want to *be* Knish.

On the other hand, it might not matter what I think. I'm out on the street by then, trying to figure it, walking the long crosstown blocks back to the apartment. The thing is, I'm a big boy, or I ought to be. I'm a grown-up. I know that everybody doesn't get to be the thing they wanted to be, the kid with the astronaut suit doesn't always get to be an astronaut, the kid with the cowboy hat ends up at an insurance company in Jersey. I look around and I see this: most people wouldn't have chosen the lives they're leading. They just ended up with them somehow, a lucky or unlucky series of accidents. And I also know that most people are okay with this. They don't get to be astronauts, they get to run the parts counter at the Chevy dealer, but still they've got their kids and their house and their gas grill and so on. I knew this is part of being a person, learning to live with this. You have a dream, and then you have a life.

But still, I don't want to end up like Knish.

I end up back at the apartment, watching Eric Seidel on video. It's the 1988 World Series of Poker, biggest tournament in the world and the moment I'm watching is when Johnny Chan has just won the whole fucking thing. I mean, he's sitting there with his arms in the air while the dealer pushes the whole stake toward him, every dollar on the table. And the whole world is watching Johnny Chan, he's a good guy, great player, you don't mind seeing him win. It's his moment. But the face I'm focused on is Eric Seidel, down in the corner of the frame. He has gotten to the final table and gotten through the last round and down to just two, him and Johnny Chan. And Johnny has just handed his ass to him. Every nickel he brought with him is sitting in front of Johnny Chan now.

Probably not what he had in mind, either.

You have a dream, you have an idea about yourself. Then the world does whatever it does to you. It goes along or it doesn't. This seems to be my lesson for the day.

I'm rewinding the tape, getting ready to watch the moment again, when the door buzzer sounds. It's fucking Worm, I know it. I don't particularly want to see him.

"Yeah?" I ask the speaker.

"Mike?" It's a woman's voice, a surprise. "It's Petra. Can I come up?"

"Sure, sure, sure," I tell her, although this is not the night I'd pick to see her, either. I buzz her in, picturing her the last time I saw her at the Taj: a dress up to here and down to there. She throws off so much freelance sex that it's hard to know if it's particularly aimed at you. Still, I have my suspicions, or my ambitions, whatever they are. I look around the apartment but it's hopeless. Pathetic. Chicks really dig a pathetic guy.

"I haven't seen the place in a while," she says, stepping through the doorway and shucking her coat and looking around in one smooth motion. "It looks . . . about the same."

She's wearing not much under her coat, and what there is is silky and close to her body.

I shrug, surrender. She brushes past me and wanders into the living room, where Johnny Chan is eyeing his cards in freeze-frame, waiting for Seidel to make his move, again.

"Eighty-eight World Series, huh?" she says, peering into the box. "Johnny Chan. Flops the nut straight, and has the discipline to wait him out. He knows Seidel's going to bluff at it."

Petra, like the rest of the world, sees this story through the eyes of Johnny Chan, winner and champion. I flip the VCR onto play again and stand there next to her, watching the screen.

"Johnny fucking Chan," I tell her.

"Look at the control," she says. "He knows his man well enough to check it all the way and risk winning nothing with those cards. He owns him."

I don't say anything, just watch the showdown unfold, move by move: Chan checks and checks, right up to the last round of bets, then sits impassively, nothing on his face, his lucky orange on the table in front of him, while Seidel makes up his mind. Finally the kid from New York decides: he goes all in, every fucking nickel, and Chan immediately covers the bet, flips his hole cards, and raises his arms in victory. The room erupts into a frenzy of shouting and cheering, every eye is on Chan and he's grinning and screaming himself, champagne bottles are going off and the babes from Binion's are starting to bring him the stacks and stacks of cash he has won, seven hundred thousand dollars total.

Meanwhile, alone in one corner of the screen, Seidel sits wondering what happened.

"Poor Seidel," Petra says. "The kid doesn't know what hit him."

I freeze the frame in midcelebration.

"I know what that feels like," I tell her, my eyes on the screen. "Gutshot. All the air rushes out of you."

She looks at me, curious, but I don't want to talk about it. Not with her anyway.

"Fuck it," I tell her, and shut the TV off. "You didn't come over here to talk about this. What's going on? You want anything? Here, sit down."

I've got the horrible couch back up out of the basement again, the one that Jo refused to have in the apartment, so at least there's something to sit on. Petra inspects it, then decides, against her better judgment, to sit anyway. Something's bothering her. She won't quite look at me.

"Tomorrow's a week," she says.

"A week of what?"

"The first two thousand you owe the Chesterfield," she says. She's watching my face, to see what I know, and I can't keep the surprise off it. I go over, fetch myself a glass of water, but it's too late: I've already tipped my hand.

"Fucking Worm," I say, more to myself than to her.

"It's a funny thing," she says—and here she's talking to me, she's telling me secrets. "He's just won eight grand. Why go on the line behind another two?"

I'm struggling to keep my cool in place. A: the fucker just beat me out of a couple of thousand dollars. B: there was only one game he could have won that eight thousand out of.

"So he beats Roman and Maurice for about eight then?" I ask her.

"Yeah," she says. "He comes back in after you leave, sits for like twenty more minutes. Then he cashes out for the full amount. Maurice hasn't been back since, Mike—I think he's been playing across the street. But Worm's been around plenty. He's run you up just under seven grand."

The number hits me hard, a body punch. Seven thousand, all on my tab. He has played me for a fool and won. Add that to the twenty-five or thirty Worm owes to Grama and Worm is a dead man, is my bet. I wonder how much of this I'll end up holding.

"Do me a favor," I tell Petra. "Put him on his own."

"Yeah?" she says. I don't know how much I've tipped to her, or how much she's guessed, but she's trying not to rub it in; she keeps her face blank, no reaction, no surprise.

"Cut him off," I say, a little more abruptly than I wanted to. I take the roll out of my pants pocket and count off a thousand and hand it to her.

"You know I just started coming around again," I tell her. "But here's a thou toward it."

She takes the money, indifferent as always. It's just a thousand. She stuffs it into her purse like a Kleenex.

She says, "Thanks for making it easy, Mike. I'm sorry to be back over here for this reason."

"Don't worry about it," I tell her.

She stands up, close. I can smell her perfume.

"I like being here," she says. "It's good to see you."

She stands a little closer: that moment when we look into each other's faces, looking for something, that answering light. But Petra's face is too long used to indifference, real or not. Whatever light she's got is buried deep. Quickly, before we lose the moment, I pull her close to me and kiss her and feel the long fine lines of her body pressed up close against my own.

But this is what's running through my head: Fucking Worm! Seven thousand dollars! Fucking Worm! Seven thousand dollars! Fucking Worm! Seven thousand dollars!

"I could stay . . ." she says; and God knows I could use a break from my own thoughts. I feel like I've been living inside my head too long, like going to the beach and it rains and rains and you're stuck inside for a week. Just sick of the fucking carpet and the wallpaper. Fucking Worm! I think. Seven thousand dollars!

"Not tonight," I tell her, and step back. We look at each other, uncertain, trying to figure what just happened or didn't happen; then the professional in us comes out, and our faces click shut again.

"I'll see you later this week, Petra," I tell her; and, without a word a glance or a touch, she gets her coat and she is gone out the door. Is she pissed? Should she be? But this will have to wait for another day.

"Fucking Worm!" I say out loud to the empty apartment.

I know where he is.

It costs me fifty-seven dollars in cab fare, all the way out to fucking New Jersey, but the way I figure it, it's just a drop in the bucket. The line of reasoning is this: I am totally, utterly, completely fucked. You can't get any more fucked than this. It's like being pregnant, you can't be more pregnant or less pregnant, you either are or you aren't. You can't be more fucked than I am. Seven thousand dollars.

I get the taxi to drop me in the middle of a dark street in front of an abandoned Catholic high school in Paterson fucking New Jersey, which bothers him a little. Not enough to keep him from taking my money. I wait till he's gone around the corner and the street is empty.

Then I pry the grille open on the ground-floor window of the ex-high school, the one I know is loose, and I let myself into the basement. It's weird inside, ghostly. It still smells of chalk dust and incense, though there's also rat piss in the mix these days, and a sour smell like wet paper bags. I make my way through the basement hallways, up through the wide staircase and into the dark gym—and in the gym, I smell tobacco smoke. I was right.

I flip the lights on all at once and call his name: "Worm!"

Nothing.

"I know you're in here," I tell him.

Nothing, again. It's weird being in here: the floors are polished, the seats around the edge are clean and empty. At one end is the stage, for assemblies and talent contests, lectures and school plays. This is the stage, in sixth grade, where the kid with the harelip won the talent show by singing "Moon River."

"Worm!" I yell again. "Get your skinny ass out here."

Casually, like he didn't hear me the first time, Worm steps out from behind the curtain.

"Hey, Mikey," he says, like he's just finding out I'm here, like he's surprised. He steps down from the stage to the gym floor, dribbling a basketball when he hits the hardwood.

"Good thing Grama doesn't know you as well as I do," I tell him.

This doesn't register at all. He sends a bounce pass in my direction by way of answer.

"Horse?" he says automatically. "Fifty bucks a letter."

"When I win, you going to pay me with my own fucking money?"

I drill the basketball straight back at him, hard as I can. I don't much care if it hits him in the face or not.

"Easy," Worm says, and tosses the ball back to me, demonstrating. "Step," he says, "and snap the thumbs down."

"Fuck you," I tell him, and shoot the ball into the dark corner of the gym, hard as I can. I'm sick of this already and we haven't even started yet.

"All right," Worm says. "We'll work on the accuracy."

This doesn't make me laugh.

"Would you stop fucking around for five minutes?" I ask him. "For once in your fucking life. You stupid, selfish prick."

"Jesus," Worm says. "You sound like my old man."

"I ought to kick the crap out of you like he did."

Worm blinks at me. This isn't joking ground, this business with his dad. I've gone a step further than I'm supposed to, which is exactly what I meant to do. He looks at me and then he looks away, goes after the basketball. But he looks back at me on the way, trying to figure me out. I've hurt him, I think. Good.

"You remember when we found this place?" he says. He's off in the corner, dribbling, shooting hoops.

"Eleventh grade," I say. "We broke in when Tommy Manzy was looking to pound you into oblivion."

"What was he pissed about, you remember?"

He puts the ball under his arm, waits for the answer.

"You fucked his mother," I tell him. I can't help myself from smiling.

"Good-looking older woman," Worm says.

"She was that," I admit, "but you spent a year dodging that sick fuck Manzy. Till he pissed off Lostrito and that garbage can fell on his head from thirty floors up."

"Crazy times," Worm says—and I get the play now, trying to suck me back into the sixth grade, the romance of it. "We were wild then."

I'm not biting. "Nothing's changed," I tell him. "You were hiding out because of your trouble then. You're still hiding out."

"I remember hiding out plenty," Worm says, peering at me across the gym like he needs glasses. "Not behind solo fuckups though. I seem to remember a running buddy."

I'm still not biting. "We got caught back then, the worst thing that could happen was you catch a beating or get expelled. Now," I tell him, "now you're fixing to go down hard. And it seems like you want to."

"I'm turning things around," Worm says; but he's not even convincing himself. "Don't you worry. No garbage can's going to hit me."

Suddenly I'm sick of this. Nothing I can say, nothing I can do is going to make a difference in his life.

"That's right," I tell him. "You're going to get out of the way and the garbage can is going to land on me. I'll see you later, Worm."

I'm on my way to the door, I'm not even looking back.

"Listen, Mike," he says. "Listen. Don't leave."

There's a pleading note in his voice that wasn't there before. The bluff and bluster vanish; and behind them, what else is there? There's no inside to him, I think. It's all outside, getting caught, getting away with it.

"I'm sorry about that money," he says, looking suitably sorry, like he was stuffed. I fucking hate it when he tries to look sincere. "Really," he says. "I needed it to get some things going."

"And?"

"I won't lie to you," Worm says. "There have been some reversals.

"How much is left?"

"Nine hundred," he says—and again, he has a hard time getting the words out, his lips twisting around the sounds. He's embarrassed. He fucking ought to be.

"You've got to be kidding," I tell him.

"I caught a frozen wave of cards like you read about," he says.

"I think I'm getting you out of hock. Instead I find out *I'm* seven grand in."

"Hey, I was feeling lucky," Worm says. "Playing blackjack over at the Horseshoe Club in Brooklyn."

This is fucking not to believed: the Horseshoe Club. The dumbest tourist in Kansas knows this isn't a straight game.

"You forgot about the Horseshoe Club?" I ask him. "The way they play the game? You schmuck."

"I thought I could neutralize them."

"*You're* fucking neutralized," I tell him. The sad-puppy looks and deep sincerity are wearing me out. I'm sick of the whole deal. I want to change channels.

"Look," I tell him, "you've really jammed me up here. Seven *grand*, Worm. I can't go any deeper, you're off the tit."

"If that's how it's got to be . . ."

I cut him off. "That's not all," I tell him. "You've got to talk to Grama, work something out."

"No way," he says. "I'm not talking to that Judas son of a bitch."

"You see any other way?" I ask him. "*Any* other way?"

I watch the combinations work their way across his face, the angles considered one by one, then dropped, re-examined, dropped again. Worm isn't dumb. His brain works fine. There's just some small part missing, I think, like the clock that runs just fine until it hits the missing cog and then it skips a second, a min-ute, an hour.

"Shit," he finally says.

"Let's get out of here," I tell him. "It's best you stay with me, for the time being."

"What, and give up the lease on my penthouse?"

"Have you got any other choices?" I ask him.

But Worm isn't done yet.

He says, "You think Manzy's mom is still around?"

Chinatown, next day, four in the afternoon. The sky is white and dirty all at once, like the sheets in a cheap motel. I knock on the door to Grama's place, a battered steel door which has been kicked in at least once before, and nothing happens.

"See?" Worm says. "Let's go."

I knock again, and this time a face appears in the reinforced-glass window—a woman's face, I guess, though it could be anything under all that makeup. She decides to let us in. The door swings open to a filthy hallway with a couple of half-naked girls in it. When she appears from behind the closing door we see that our hostess is wearing some Kmart lingerie and nothing else.

"Hi, boys," she says, a faint Russian accent.

"Hello," I tell her.

"You cops? You look like cops."

"We're not cops," Worm says, disgusted. This is the first time anybody's mistaken him for a cop in his life.

"You want a twirl then?" asks the hostess.

"No, thanks," I tell her quickly. Of all the things in the world I might desire, an hour with her is about dead last. She's maybe forty, beat-up and bruised under the makeup, with a face that could cut glass. She looks like she might have a Kazakh tank battalion or two in her past somewhere.

"Grama here?" I ask her.

"Shit," she says. We've ruined her day.

"Tell him Mike and Worm need a minute," I tell her.

She gives me one last dirty look and heads for another steel door at the end of the hallway, knocking before she goes in, closing it emphatically behind her.

"This is not good," Worm says. "I feel like I've been remanded again. You sure—"

But I cut him off.

"Don't talk so much," I tell him, nodding toward the whore down the hallway. She's talking on the phone in some other language but she could be listening. "Don't let him read your mail."

Worm looks around. He doesn't like it here. He's got that kid-outside-the-principal's-office look, not guilty because he's done something bad, just apprehensive because he is about to get his ass whipped. Which he might be, I think. Which we both might be. For about the four-hundredth time I remind myself that this is none of my doing and none of my business and I should be home asleep, anywhere but here.

"Okay," the hostess calls from the end of the hallway. We go to our punishment, muffled grunts and squeals coming from behind the various closed doors. The hostess lets us in, then goes out herself, shutting the door quickly behind her.

The reason for all this door-slamming is a pair of pit bulls Grama has wandering the mess of his office. They're a mangy light brown, no neck at all, and as the lead one comes up sniffing my crotch and drooling I try to remember what I read about the bite force they can generate. I swear to God the muscles of his jaw go straight down into his chest.

"Hey, Mike," Grama says.He's enjoying the hell out of this, one dog per crotch, grinning from someplace behind his beard—a little Charlie Parker number that looks like it crawled onto his face and died there. Grama's got the general build of a fire hydrant in a porkpie hat and his little pig eyes radiate dumb.

"Hey, Worm," he says, "it's good you came. Real smart thinking."

"Thanks for the endorsement," Worm says.

"Grama," I tell him. "It's been a long time."

He doesn't pay any attention to me at all, just dives in after Worm. "So," he says, "you brought him along to help carry all my money?"

Worm opens his mouth but I step in front of him to shut him up.

"There's no money today," I tell Grama.

The place gets quiet, quick. His little pig eyes narrow at me, like he can't believe I just said what I said. Even the dogs shut up for a second.

"No money?" Grama says, like he can't believe his ears. He looks at my face, then at Worm. He explains, "There has to be some money."

"None," Worm says. He lights a cigarette and he's expecting to get hit, I can see it in his movements, like a dog that jumps away from your hand. They say this is the most dangerous kind.

"You owe twenty-five," Grama says, still boring into Worm, "and you bring me a fucking story."

"Five grand, in a week," I tell him, stepping in between them. "You keep the juice going."

"Shut up," Grama says, holding his finger in the air, and I shut up and so does Worm. In the silence that follows, we can hear one of the dogs chewing on something. Then it stops.

"Quiet," Grama whispers. "You have to catch them in the act."

We stand there, absolutely still for a couple of seconds, Larry, Moe, and Curly Joe. I have no fucking idea what Grama is up to.

Then, quietly, the sound of chewing starts again, and Grama pounces. He falls on the nearest dog like a sandbag from the sky, flipping the dog over on his back in one quick motion, shoving the whole of his fat face into the air in front of the dog's face so that the dog sees nothing but Grama.

"Bad dog!" he says intently. "Baaad dog!"

The dog does nothing, doesn't move, doesn't make a sound. He just quietly pisses all over himself. The trickle runs off his belly and onto the filthy floor. Either Grama doesn't notice or Grama doesn't care. He gets up off the floor himself and the dog slinks away, trying to make himself invisible.

Grama says, "You can't let them get away with it, or they think they run the place. Now, where were we?"

"Jesus Christ," Worm says.

I step in front of him, shut him up again.

"Five grand," I say. "One week."

Grama draws himself up and squares his shoulders, staring me down with his little pig eyes. This is supposed to make him look impressive, I think. He's not hard to read: he read someplace that he ought to get respect, so that's what he wants. Maybe he saw it in a movie. But respect is the one thing he's never going to get from Worm. This is going to have to be my job.

"Come on," I tell him. "We want what you want—to square this thing. Three days is impossible, you know that. Five grand this week, the rest after that. No one's arguing that you're the man. Let's make it a business decision."

Grama likes this. You can see him swelling up, especially when I tell him he's the man. He's been waiting his whole life for those words. Then he notices that Worm is paying no attention to him at all, that he's watching the dogs instead, and I start to lose him.

"Look," I tell him, pleading, "Worm just got out. Put him on a plan . . ."

But Grama's had enough.

"This isn't The Money Store," he says. "We aren't negotiating here. I tell you how it works."

This stops up Worm, gets him looking at Grama again, who looks completely happy with himself, the big guy.

"This isn't fucking Burger King," he says. "You don't get it your way. You get it my way or fuck you."

"Come on," I say to him, "come on, Grama—I'm asking here."

This makes him even happier. In his dreams, everybody comes to him, kisses the ring.

"You're looking for grace," he says, like he's talking to himself. "You're looking for charity . . ."

Got him, I think: I found the spot. But Worm can't keep his trap shut."

"Charity?" he yells out. "Fucking charity? I'll rot in hell before I'll take any charity from this fat fuck of an errand boy."

"Shut the fuck up, Worm," I tell him.

But the damage is done. At the words *errand boy* I can see

Grama shrink again, small and mean and pig-eyed. Now he's going to hit somebody.

"Too late for him to shut up," Grama says. "Too fucking late. He ain't getting out of here now."

He starts for Worm but I cut him off.

"Come on," I tell him. "He's a stupid fuck but he's good for it. He'll get you your money."

Tough moment. He knows I'm being reasonable but he doesn't like me for it. Something in him, about ninety percent of what's in him, just wants to fuck somebody up. I'll do, Worm would be better. But there's also some tiny flickering of intelligence that knows that twenty-five is twenty-five and Worm won't be coming up with any of it from a hospital bed. Also there's this: when Worm told me about this little problem, he also told me Grama was working on his own in a completely sincere voice, looking into my eyes—which meant he was lying his ass off. It occurs to me that whoever he's working for might not like it if Grama took Worm out; no matter how much he'd enjoy it.

Grama spits on the floor between him and Worm. Then turns to me.

He says, "If you're saying he's good for it, Mike, it's on you, too."

It's a question. He waits for the answer. Twenty-five to this pig-eyed motherfucker plus seven to the Chesterfield, plus who knows what else. If I had any brains, I'd let Worm rot. It isn't even a question of loyalty anymore but a question of impossibility.

On the other hand . . .

On the other hand, Grama is going to fuck him up before we leave if I don't vouch for him. I've seen his work before: heavy on the muscle and careless. This one guy, Avi Zildjian, he's still in the hospital. It doesn't help that he's pissed off. I don't think

Grama would want Worm messed up to the point where he couldn't work it off—and I'm sure whoever he's working for, if there is somebody, wouldn't like it—but that doesn't mean that Grama won't get carried away in the heat of the moment.

So that's my choice: vouch for Worm or watch him get pulped. And I can't stand to watch him get hurt, no matter how richly he deserves it. So what it comes down to is no choice at all.

"Then it's on me, too," I tell Grama.

He looks surprised, and a little disappointed. He wasn't expecting this.

"Fifteen large, five days," he says. "Else I start breaking things."

"I hear you."

"In that case, you can leave," he says, and goes over to the door and unlocks it, from the inside, with a key. I didn't realize we were locked in. I wonder, as we leave, how close we came to the real thing. Two on one—he must have been carrying. One false step, I think, just one . . .

The steel door slams shut behind us and we're on our way out and the air in the hallway, despite the fact that it stinks of sweat and smoke and spermicidal jelly, is sweeter than the office, a hundred percent sweeter. The bored whore is still on the phone, the famous Natasha sits in her negligee in a folding chair by the door. She doesn't move a muscle as we go out. Monkey demon, I think, passing her. Beware the monkey demon.

Out on the street, I start to giggle.

"You fucking almost got killed in there," I say to Worm.

But he doesn't want to talk. He's in his own private bad mood, and I have to hurry to follow him as he races off toward Canal Street. It started to rain a little while we were inside, and all the headlights are on now—late afternoon, rain, headlights. I follow him through the smells of diesel smoke and shrimp and incense, the sound of spoken Cantonese and Chinese disco.

"I can't believe I'm going out like this," he says.

"Like what?"

"Fifteen grand in five days," he says, stopping to talk under a greengrocer's awning. "Forget it, man, we're done."

"We're not done yet," I tell him. "Fifteen grand? I've gone on rushes that big before."

"Come on, Mike," he says. The boy behind the cash register is giving us a dirty look for taking up his space and I'm wondering who is bullshitting who here. I'm not fooling Worm anyway.

"Maybe under optimum conditions," he says. "Maybe. But how much do you have on you?"

"Three-fifty," I admitted.

"That puts us at twelve hundred. What do you think we can do with that? Fucking play Lotto?"

"We do what we do," I tell him.

This takes a minute to sink in; and then I see a kind of joy light up in his eyes, just like old times, I think, that's all he wants—just like old times.

"Like in Princeton?" he says hopefully.

"We can't sit together," I tell him. "This isn't that big of a city for somebody to figure it out. No, we'll do it like we used to. You find the games, you scout the games. I sit and mop them up."

"Fuck," he says, and looks around at the rain. We're the only people under the awning and the boy is still staring at us. When Worm looks back, I can see his eyes are real, for a change. This is really happening, for a change. It isn't just a game.

"You'd still do that for me," he says.

"No fucking choice, buddy," I tell him. "I'm hanging on the hook right next to you."

I reach into his shirt pocket and pull out his smokes, shake one out, and stick it in the corner of my mouth. Then I put the pack back in his pocket.

"You want a light?" he says.

"Not yet," I tell him. "Not till this shit blows up and we're riding the dog down to Baltimore. Meanwhile, we got work to do. The ones I already figure are the thirty-sixty at the Chesterfield, especially if Greggie is still sitting—"

"He's not anymore," Worm says.

"Then there's the Greeks, the union game, the four A.M. over in Woodside. You find me some more."

"You sure you ready for this?"

"Lead me to it," I tell him. "Five days."

"Fuck, yes," he says. "Let's go. Let's play some cards."

Sixty-four hours later . . .

Sixty-four hours later I am still awake, more or less, and I am sitting in the bar of the Swan Meadows Golf Course, watching the rain pour down outside on all that bright green chemical lawn and wishing I was out there somewhere in the cold, clean rain. Instead I am sitting with the membership, a couple of caddies, and the club pros, playing seven stud with the deuces wild. This was my grandmother's favorite game. Next stop, Acey-Deucey.

My mouth tastes like an ashtray and the insides of my eyeballs are sanded and raw. There are little prickles of light at the edges of my vision. None of this matters because there is money on the table, and lots of it. Most of it used to belong to the members; most of it now belongs to two of us, myself and Johnny Gold, the pro. I'm waiting on him. At some point he's going to go ballistic, I know it—and we're playing pot limit, so if I can get him going, I can turn him in one hand. I'm waiting for the hand is all. It's hard, because I want to get it over with. I'm running out of gas, and my head is buzzing with the games and the games and the games: Larossa folding a pat hand under my nothing at the Union Hall; Zagosh missing his straight by one number at the Chesterfield; Zizzo and Taki screaming their idiot heads off at each other in the Neptune Diner; worst of all, the fucking yuppie game at the cigar store in Woodside, ten players and nine cigars, everybody but me. I smelled like a fucking *robusto derelicto* coming out of that one but I had their money, yes I did. A river of cards, games, hands, faces. It's getting late, it's getting harder to sort out what's here from what was yesterday and that is not a good frame of mind to be in when you're trying to take somebody's money.

"What the hell," says Johnny Gold, the pro. "It's only money. I'll bet."

I've got two pair myself, kings over eights. Not exactly invulnerable. He's got nothing showing, but with the wild cards in there, it's impossible to tell.

"Then let's get some more money in there," I tell him. "Make it five hundred."

Johnny Gold makes that little move with his mouth and I know—I *know*—he hasn't got it. But then this little voice starts up: are you sure? what if he does? what about those fucking deuces?

"All right," says Johnny Gold. "I raise. Size of the pot."

Worm is suddenly right behind me, counting the money on the table along with me: fifteen hundred, maybe two thousand. I can cover the bet, no problem.

His pal, Weitz, says to Johnny Gold, "You sure on that, Goldie? You might want to leave some over for your daughter's riding lessons."

Then I think: this isn't my time. My time is coming but this isn't it.

"Take it down," I tell Gold, and muck my cards in with the others.

Gold is grinning, ear to ear. He turns his cards, although nobody has called him: nothing.

"Look at that," he says, high-fiving Weitz. "I bluffed out the ringer. What do you know about that?"

He grins at me as he pulls in the pot and I make my mental note: make this one painful, when his time comes. He's acting about as badly as it's possible to behave. I'm going to pull the wings off this one slow.

"Come on," Worm says in my ear. "Let's go."

I look up at him, shake him off, but he insists. My time is coming. Why can't he see it?

"Come on," he says again, and this time I let him. I gather the cash off the table in front of me, tip my hat to the others, and walk out. I'm fucking retreating. This is wrong. As I go out I can hear Gold bragging behind me.

"What do I always say?" he says. "Anybody, anywhere, anytime . . ."

"What the fuck is the matter with you?" Worm asks, as soon as we're in the car.

"I didn't have it," I tell him.

"You didn't have it?" Worm says. "Since when do you got to have it to beat a puke like that out of a pot? A grade-schooler would have played back at him."

I don't have much to say. The rain comes down across the windshield, the clean spring rain. Worm is right, as far as he goes—I mean, I would have taken the pot, would have taken Gold down, almost all the way. I just had an instinct. And instincts are all I have, all I can trust.

"I was prepared to wait him out," I tell Worm. "Eventually he'd have bluffed at the wrong pot, and I'd have had him."

"Eventually, shit," Worm says. "We don't have the time. You've got to make your moves."

"The move was folding," I tell him. "You can't lose what you don't put in the middle."

"Fuck that," Worm says; draws back and starts to study my face, trying to figure where I'm at. In the rainy afternoon light, he looks like seven kinds of shit. I don't imagine I look any better. Maybe I am starting to lose it, the edge I need. I can't tell. The thing is about losing your edge, you can't tell when it goes.

"We needed that pot," Worm says. "Where are we at anyway?"

"You count it," I say, flipping him the roll. "I'm too tired."

"Too tired to count money," he says, slipping the rubber band off, fanning out the green. "That's bad." He sorts it with a practiced hand, slipping the bills around so they're all the same way, faces up and to the left.

"Seventy-three hundred," he announces when he's done. "That pot you just gave that V-neck sweater would have put us near ten grand. Look at you, you're going senile on me. One sixty-four hour session and you need a nap."

A nap! The word itself sounds sweet to me. The idea of a little daytime sleeping, even with the pillow drooling and the weird dreams, sends chills down my neck. Suddenly my head feels like it weighs as much as it actually does, a big skin bag of water and weird junk.

"Fuck that," I tell him. "We don't have the time. I'll sleep when I'm dead."

"Don't say that," Worm says, staring out the window at the falling rain. "Don't fucking say that."

"What's next?" I ask him.

"Seventy-three hundred," Worm says, laying it out for himself. "We got two days to double it."

It doesn't sound too likely, sitting there in the rain. In fact, it sounds impossible, not with my brain in the kind of leaky shape it's in and all the easy games cleaned out. Maybe Worm was right in Chinatown. Maybe we should be riding the dog out of town, far the fuck away from here and fast. California's nice this time of year, they say.

"Look, I've got an idea," Worm says.

I don't answer him for a second. Some of the worst experiences of my life have started with those very words. The thing about Worm's ideas is that they never sound as bad as they turn out; they always seem sort of reasonable and workable and there's always an angle he forgot to tell you about. You never find this out until it's too late.

On the other hand, we're about forty-six hours from the Greyhound station. I'm willing to listen.

"A game?" I ask him.

"It's in Binghamton, is the problem. But it's big—twelve or sixteen guys, municipal workers, they come in after payday and they play all night. Two tables."

"Yeah, but we kill five hours each way driving. We don't have the time."

Worm shrugs. "You could sleep on the way up," he says. "Maybe get half your brain back. You were looking pretty worthless in there."

"I had a plan."

"Whatever," Worm says. "Either that, or you could let me come in and give you a hand in there." He nods toward the clubhouse. "There's money on the table in there," he says. "You wouldn't mind seeing Johnny Gold eat a little shit, would you?"

"Not that way."

"Picky motherfucker," Worm says. "It's up to you."

I think about it for a minute; but the prospect of a few hours of sleep—even sleep in a moving car, with Worm behind the wheel, no less—is more than I can resist. It's weakness, I know it. I'll pay for it later.

"Binghamton it is," I tell him. "Wake me up when we get to the parking lot."

"Sweet dreams," says Worm. "You want to stop, get a blanket or something? Either that or I bet I could go back in there and kype one from someplace."

"My coat is fine," I tell him. "My coat is beautiful."

I leave the keys in the ignition and me and Worm do a Chinese firedrill, him ending up behind the wheel and me stretched out in the backseat. It's weird to watch as we start out, the way the trees zip by outside the windows, the way you can't see any cars or buildings, just sky and trees and wires and birds. It reminds me of being a kid, the way you trusted your parents to drive and you could do any fucking thing you wanted. Now, when I drive with somebody else, I'm always watching, anticipating. I feel like I need to take responsibility. Not today though—today I lay back and feel the push and shove of the engine, the tug of the brakes, watch the wires go by outside the window and listen to Worm, searching the dial for a radio station he can stand. I can feel myself slipping, going. Something in me tries to fight it. Not for long.

I'm on the train again, dreaming, the lights going by and nobody behind the wheel. I always wake up before the end of the tunnel. Twice—once in daylight and the second time after dark—I wake up full of fear, my feet trying to bust out the door. Somebody told me once if you die in your dreams, you die for real. I doubt it, but I've never died. The second time, it takes me a while to get back to sleep, lying there watching the headlights play across the head-liner of the car, the shadows and light and speed. It all comes together with my dream, the lights between stations, and I don't even realize I'm asleep again until we pass through the station, all lit up, neon and tile, the passengers watching as the train blows right through without them, not even slowing . . .

"Mike," somebody calls out. "Mike?"

"What the fuck?"

"We're here."

It takes me a long time, maybe a minute or more, to figure out where *here* is and who is talking to me and so on. The dream bleeds into my memory so that I can't quite tell if the cigar store game was real or not.

"Time is it?" I ask him, sitting up.

"Eleven," he tells me. "A little after."

My neck is stiff, my mouth is dry, there's junk in my head and junk in my eyes. Plus we're in fucking Binghamton. Something about the trees.

"I got you a Eggamuffin," Worm says. "Shot of coffee. Good as new."

"How are you doing?"

"Well, you know."

"What?"

"I'm seeing some shit by the side of the road that isn't there. But basically, okay."

He passes the McDonald's bag back into the backseat and I sit there huddled against the window, eating the sandwich, watching Binghamton roll by outside the window. It's a depressing sight, quiet, cold. There's nobody on the street, outside of cars. The sandwich is greasy, hot, strange—it's not quite like recognizable human food—but the coffee is okay. I'm still half-stuck in the dreamworld, where things in your head have reality and weight. I'm thinking about the apartment, before Jo left, and it's like I can touch it—the nice furniture, the fucking coffeemaker, striped sheets on the beds, and matching towels. That's what I left to come here. There must be something wrong with me, I think. I must be fucking crazy.

"Drink up," says Worm. "Get that coffee circulating. We're going to make some money tonight."

We're almost outside of town when he turns into a parking lot. B.P.O.E. 1157, says the sign—the Benevolent and Protective Order of Elks. He pulls up in front of an antique brick building that looks something like a prison, except a little more run-down and not nearly so cheerful. We pull into the parking lot end every car in the parking lot is the same.

"Oh, shit," I tell Worm.

Every car in the parking lot is a brown-and-white from the Highway Patrol. This is a cop game. This is the part that Worm left out.

"Municipal workers, huh?" I ask him.

"Well, they work for the city."

"They work for the state," I tell him. "I don't like this. I don't like this at all."

"You see any other outs?" he asks.

I sit there, looking at the dozen cop cars. I'm going to play with them and beat them, here, two hundred and fifty miles from home.

"You could have told me," I say to Worm.

"You wouldn't have come."

"I don't get a choice in this?"

"You've got a choice," he says. "Right now. Either we bust this game, right now, tonight, or we get our asses over to the bus station and get the fuck out of Dodge. There isn't another game that can get us out of this. Not that I know of."

I turn this over in my mind for a while, without liking it any better. The thing is, I can't see where he's wrong.

I ask him, "How am I even supposed to get into this game?"

"Easy," Worm says. "This guard, Pete Frye, I must have lost ten grand to him over eighteen months. This guy thought I was tuna fish. His nephew plays here. Ask for Sean Frye."

I don't like this, I think, not one bit. But there's no way around it.

"I figure about eight hours," I tell Worm—and I watch his little face light up with glee, he's getting what he wants, things are going his way. "You can be back here by what? seven, seven-thirty in the morning."

"What the hell am I going to do in this town for eight hours? All they have is car washes and liquor stores."

"No, Worm," I tell him, before he even asks.

"I just thought I'd come in," he says. "Sit for a while."

"Look around you," I tell him, waving my arm toward the fleet of identical brown-and-whites. "We'd have to be nuts to walk in there together. I'm about half-ready to give it up anyway."

"Come on," he says. "I'll play it straight up."

"Fine," I tell him, suddenly sick of his bullshit. He's gotten me to Binghamton, he's gotten me into the cop game, now he wants to fuck me up completely. I feel like I've lost track somewhere, that I've let go of things I shouldn't have.

"Fine," I tell him. "You go in, you play, and I'll be back in eight hours, okay?"

Worm lights a cigarette. I don't know if he's actually thinking about this or whether he's just giving me a pause for dramatic

143

effect. I don't know if Worm does anything that could legitimately be described as *thinking,* to tell you the truth. It's like some demented pinball machine in there.

And here I am in Binghamton . . .

"Okay okay okay," he finally says. "I'll find a bowling alley or something. Go get 'em."

Before he goes, I reach into his pocket again, slip his pack out, and steal one of his cigarettes—for luck, all for luck. I stick it into my mouth but I don't light it. Not yet. Things are not quite bad enough yet. We're getting there though.

I get a bad feeling as soon as I get inside. It's a long, low, dim room with wood paneling on the walls, deer heads and beer signs, a vinyl-covered bar in Italian pimp red, red electrician's tape covering the cracks. What is it about Upstate? There's something depressing in the light, in the color and the air of the place, something that failed a while ago but is still pissed-off about it. The cops are at the far end, two tables of them, as promised. They look like sides of beef with shirts on, big stumpy bastards. It's a heads-down, serious game. There's money in the room, I can feel it.

"Can I help you?" asks the bartender.

Run away, I think, looking into his face—big dead eyes set into a moon of fat, a softball bat behind the counter somewhere, maybe a thirty-eight. They know how to take care of trouble here. One false move, one missed step . . . but it's too late anyway, the thing has been decided and it's either this or Grama. And at least with this, I've got a chance.

"I'm looking for Sean Frye," I tell the bartender.

"That's him over there," the bartender says, still suspicious, pointing to a goof in a sports-car hat at one of the tables. I can feel his eyes on me as I cross the dark room over to the tables, the circle of light and the green felt and the snap and rattle of cards.

"Sean Frye?" I ask him.

"What do you want with him?" asks the goof, looking up, hard-faced.

I tell him, "Your Uncle Pete said to ask for you if I was ever up near here."

He's still suspicious.

"You one of his students?" he asks.

"No," I tell him, trying to sell it. "I wasn't inside."

"You must know him from hunting then."

I can't decide if this is a trap or not. I don't have any idea whether his uncle is a hunter or a ballet dancer. In the second before I answer, I scan his face and decide: he's open, he's honest, he's all right.

"He beat me for about a grand over at the lodge," I tell him. "Your uncle did."

Right answer.

"That's the buy-in here," Sean Frye says. "Twenty-forty stud is the game. Take a seat. What's your name, anyway?"

"Mike," I tell him. "Mike Silvretti."

"Fellas, this is Mike," says Sean—not that there's any need to, they've all been watching me with both eyes since I walked up to the table. These are big boys but they're jumpy as cats. As soon as Sean introduces me, though, they all back down. They mumble, "Hey, hello, how you doin'?" and bend their thick necks to the card game again.

I ease down into the game, never quite letting my guard fall. These are cops, after all. Not that I've got anything against them. It's just that about three-quarters of the stuff I enjoy doing in my life, including what I'm doing right now, happens to be completely illegal. It's always made me nervous to be around them, and at first it's the same way here.

As the hours pass—midnight, one in the morning, two—I start to let my own defenses down a little. These are hard guys, sure, but there's a softer side to them you don't see. It shows in the little things. They ask about one another's relatives, one another's kids. They shoot the breeze between hands about the girls they went to high school with, girls that have turned into mothers, married some of these guys, married some other guys. There's this one girl, Dorothy, that they talk about—a high school honey, I guess, fallen on hard times, trailer houses and spouse abuse and kids. They've got a plan for keeping the husband in line. What they can't do is keep her from going back to them. They can't figure it. They stare blank-eyed into this mystery for a while and I like them for it. Between them, they've got a picture of a whole place, all the people in it. I'm jealous of them, in a weird way. Beneath all this hard shell—the tough faces, the angry bartender—is a soft center. These guys have known one another since grade school, the way I have with Worm. But instead of the I-me-mine that I've been living by, these guys have been out taking care of the people around them, taking care of one another. Listening to them talk about Mrs. This and Old Man That and the night shift down in Cracktown, I think: this is something I will never have, this feeling, holding a whole place inside your mind and knowing it and belonging there . . .

On the other hand, this soft center makes for some very lousy cardplaying. In general, the rule is: the nicer the guy, the poorer the cardplayer. These cops are no exception. They can't even keep themselves covered up. They're showing me their fucking cards, though I don't dare look, and I don't need to. They're wearing every fucking hand on their faces, plain as day. It's like playing

Indian poker. Three or four hours into it, we're getting along fine, everybody's happy, I'm up forty-two hundred and counting the minutes till morning. This is cake.

Until . . .

Three-fifteen in the goddamned morning and everything's going fine and then I hear the door open up behind me and slam shut again and I know something is about to go wrong. I'm sitting with my back to the door and I can't stand to look, not at first. My tablemates all glance up and I can see it's somebody familiar.

"Hey, Bear," says the guy to my right, Vitter.

And Sean Frye says, "Hey, Bear."

And I turn and there's a large cop-looking guy just coming up to the tables and there, right behind him, is Worm.

"Hey, fellas," Bear says to the two tables. "I met this guy down at the tavern. He says he likes to play a little cards."

"Well, he came to the right place," Vitter says, scraping his chair along the wood floor to make a place for him. With Bear to vouch for him, there's no hesitation to let Worm in. He is welcomed with open arms.

"Sean Frye," says Sean Frye, holding his hand out to shake. "This is Vitter, Whitley, Osbourne. And this guy's name is Mike."

Worm is shaking hands with everybody, like he's running for fucking Congress, and when he gets to me I look him in the eye and think: you stupid, selfish prick. Three-and-a-half more hours and we would have been home free. I don't know what's going to happen next but I know it's something. Something's coming.

"I'm Les," Worm says, pumping away.

"Deal Les a hand," says Vitter.

At first he plays it straight. He sees—he *must* see—that I'm doing fine without him, and the first hour or so is difficult on the nerves, but okay. He deals in turn, nothing too amazing happens, no rabbits, no hats. I even start to relax a little, thinking maybe I underestimated Worm. Maybe he can see a good thing, see when enough is enough, lay off the obvious shit and be content to make our nickel and go home. He's a little behind but not nearly enough to put a dent in what I've won so far. Still, this worries me: Worm would only let himself get behind in a game like this if he was sandbagging. I can't help thinking of the Princeton game. I win some, I lose some. I'm finding it a little hard to concentrate.

Maybe it's time to go, I think. Cash out and check out. A few hard feelings from the officers, but as long as I obey the speed limit . . .

It's Worm's deal, seven stud. My first up card is the king of hearts, with Officer Osbourne showing an ace. I take a look at my hole cards: king of spades, king of clubs. Fucking Worm, I think. You fucking fucked-up fuckhead Worm.

"Ace bets," says Worm, and I wonder what he's set up: a pair of aces under my kings maybe. Either that or something really blatant and stupid like a full house.

"I like what I've got," Osbourne says. "I'll go twenty."

"I believe you," I tell him. "I fold."

And the hand goes on and nobody's looking and Worm gives me one quick pissed-off look and then on with it. He's pissed at me for folding his trick. What's going on is what I was afraid of: in his hour at the table, Worm has finally realized what a soft game this is underneath. It's like he can't help himself. Or maybe he really can't, maybe he really is broken this way, I think. It doesn't matter at this point. Get out, I think, run away. Get your little ass out of there in one piece.

But we're still thirty-five hundred short, give or take, and there's money in the room. Maybe Worm will knock it off. Maybe he just had the one stunt in mind. If he can just lay off, I can get enough out of this bunch to straighten out Grama.

I play around the table, everybody dealing in turn, and before every hand I feel like I should get out. All I have to do is push back the chair, stand up, grin, and shake some hands. One chance, I think, looking at Worm. One more chance and that's all you get.

It comes around to Worm's deal. I get an ace up, the high card showing. But when I look in the hole, a pair of sevens sit there looking up at me. Worm has done it again.

"Check," I say, easy as I can. I don't want to mark this for the cops. What I'm doing is waiting for somebody to bet so I can fold gracefully, cash out and good-bye.

Not one of these bastards will bet though. The thing checks all the way around. There's no way out till the next card.

And, as Worm deals the next card, a giant cop hand reaches out and grabs Worm by the wrist, just as he has dealt me my third seven.

"Hold on there a fucking second," says Vitter, the cop belonging to the hand.

Everything just falls off the table. Nobody talks, everybody watches, both tables.

"Put the deck down," Vitter says.

"What?" says Mr. Innocent.

"Put the fucking deck down," Vitter says.

Worm slowly lowers the deck onto the table.

"Trouble, Stu?" asks Sean Frye.

"It looks like we've got ourselves a road gang here."

Everybody from the other table gets up and gathers around, a circle of solid mean. The world narrows to this one table, this one light, and at the center of it is a deck of cards, and two hands, mine and Worm's. But there's nothing wrong with Worm's. I know that already. It's my little sevens that lie there, face down, with the third seven and the ace on top.

"What the hell is going on, Stu?" asks one of the players from the other table. I assume he's an officer in the patrol. He certainly seems ready to take charge.

Vitter says, "This son of a bitch was base dealing and caught a hanger."

The bottom two cards, it's true, are sticking out from the deck at a slight angle. Still.

"Base dealing?" says Mr. Innocent. "Hanger? What the fuck are you talking about?"

Shut up, I think. Shut up and quit cheating. I might as well say it in Chinese.

The officer tells him, "What he's saying is that you're dealing from the bottom of the deck."

Worm looks up into the lights, into the officer's face. He's never heard of such a thing.

Sean Frye says, "What did he give him?"

"Seven of hearts," says Visser.

The officer turns to me. I'm sitting, he's standing, his face just coming through the edge of the light. He's done this kind of thing before. He's talked to a few suspects.

"Are you boys professionals?" he asks me. "Are you working us?"

"No, look—" I start, but he cuts me off with a wave of his hand.

"Don't answer," says the officer. "Your cards will speak for you now. As long as that seven didn't help you, we'll listen to what you have to say. Turn his cards, Whitley."

Whitley flips them, and there they lie: seven of clubs, seven of spades. They lie there on the green felt looking unnaturally bright and clear, like you could see them from a mile off, like they've got some kind of a light of their own. There's a moment's quiet surprise, a little pang of sorrow in my own chest. They *liked* me. We were getting along fine. They can't quite believe, not at first, that I came to cheat them.

It's very quiet. Something's about to happen.

The officer says, "One last thing."

He reaches for the deck, there on the table, and turns it over and shakes his head and then he shows the bottom card to the rest of the boys: ace of diamonds.

Still the quiet goes on, just more concentrated, the spotlight down on us. Everybody's eyes are on us. Worm can't resist the opportunity. There's something broken in him. Now's a good time for a joke, he thinks.

"Well, boys," he says brightly. "I guess you'll be reading us our rights, then."

He looks up, grins, and every hand in the place starts against us. My chair goes out from under me first, a fist to the side of the face at the same time and after than I'm on the floor, holding my hands against the back of my neck, curling, tight as I can, into a little ball on the floor while the fists come raining down. Then they start kicking. A black shoe jars my hand loose from my face and the next one lands on my eye, the sharp blunt toe of a boot, and another before I can get covered up again. Nothing hurts yet, or at least not as bad as it will. There's the fear. These guys aren't in their regular minds. Boys together like this, anything can happen, events can get carried away with themselves, there's no knowing how far they might go. For a second I see myself in the roadside shallow grave, the lonesome grave off in the woods, and then my hand comes loose and somebody grinds it into the floor and then, mysteriously, it stops. I feel a practiced hand going through my pockets, stripping them of every cent.

Then they haul me to my feet and shuffle me toward the open door—the bartender is holding it for them—and shove me out into the gravel of the parking lot. For a second, I think I might make it standing. But then a black well opens up at my feet, an elevator shaft without a bottom, full of bright stars.

i come around some time later, I don't know when. At first I just lie there with my eyes closed. Now this has started to hurt. My side hurts, my face, my hand where they stood on it, and inside of my gut is the feeling that something is really wrong. The inside and the outside of my body feel like different sizes. My spleen, I think. I knew a guy, back in the city, they beat him up so bad one time in a robbery that they had to go in and take his spleen out. Afterward he was just fine. None of the doctors ever quite told him what a spleen was or why he needed one, when he got along so well without one. They just explained how big it was, and how full of blood.

And something in me likes this.

Something in me thinks: You deserve this, for all the foolish things you have done to get here. I have violated the laws of sanity and self-preservation and reasonableness. I could perfectly well

153

be sitting on the sofa of a well-lit apartment, boning up on my torts while a beautiful naked woman sleeps in the next room. Instead I am lying cheek-to-gravel in the parking lot of an Elks Club in Binghamton. None of this would be possible without my stupidity, my arrogance. This is my punishment. I remember the words of the Mass: My fault, my fault, my most grievous fault . . .

Remember this, I tell myself. Remember this moment. You need to take better care of yourself.

Then I think: It doesn't matter. I remember the practiced hand going through my pockets, and then I remember that the seventy-three hundred is gone and the thirty-five hundred I was up and the change for the parking meter besides. Fucked, flustered, and far from home. My own weakness makes me sick.

I sit up, cautiously, look around. My head spins and then it holds, comes up straight. The parking lot is empty except for the rent-a-car, that and a bag of clothes, twenty feet away, that I know to be Worm. Maybe he's dead, I think. Maybe I'll kill him if he's not.

I don't dare stand, not yet, but I do manage to crawl over to the body and he's not moving at all. I watch his shoulders for breathing and I don't see any. His leather jacket is scuffed and torn from the gravel. I don't know if this is going to matter or not.

"Worm," I whisper sharply. "Worm!"

Nothing.

"Les!" I say to him. I don't even know why I'm whispering. I reach out—cowardly, in case I'm touching a dead man—and gently shake his shoulder, trying to bring him around.

"Worm!"

"Oh . . ." he says. He rolls over onto his back, his face to the sky, eyes closed. He groans out "Mike . . ."

"What?"

154

"Mike . . ."

"Are you okay?"

"Mike," he says. "You should have played the kings, Mike."

I look down at him, and for a second I think I want to kill him, and then I crack up, I can't help it. Worm laughs, too, although I can tell it hurts him. He scrunches up on one side, holding his ribs while he giggles. Good, I think. It hurts you, too.

"You asshole," I tell him.

"I know, I know," he says. Still lying there, he opens his eyes, blinks. Then automatically he goes to his pockets, patting them in turn. Nothing. He looks up at me.

"Everything," I tell him. "They got it all."

Worm sits up, shakes his head to clear the stars and rockets. He looks like he's going to stand up but he doesn't quite. Instead he contorts himself around to slip his right boot off—I can tell this hurts him, too—and shakes out three damp bills onto the gravel.

"Three hundred," he says. "That's all I got."

I feel around for the cigarette pack in my shirt pocket. The cigarettes are all broken naturally, but the folded-up hundred is still there. It takes me a while to work it out of the pack, though, with my fingers in the kind of shape they are. I spit on the gravel, and it comes out red: blood.

Worm lights a cigarette in three tries.

Now, I think. Now's as good a time as any.

"Give me one of those, would you?" I ask him. "And give me a light while you're at it."

Worm looks over, impressed. He hands me a cigarette and his lighter, one of those tiny Bic jobs, and I see the problem with this tiny lighter and beat-up hands. It takes me a while to find the little wheel, turn it, get the thing lit.

"I can't believe I caught a fucking hanger," Worm says. "That never happens."

It's just words though. That's what I have finally figured out about Worm: it's all just words, none of it matters. I take a long drag off the cigarette and, when I inhale it, start to cough like a motherfucker. It's one of those coughs that starts down deep in my belly, that takes every one of my bruised ribs to get out. The pain is amazing. When it stops, after a minute, I sit there staring at the cigarette. I thought you were my friend, I think. The pain is still amazing.

"Those guys were thorough," I say. "Anything broken on you?"

"Maybe my nose," he says.

I toss the cigarette, still lit, into a patch of diseased bushes at the edge of the lot. Another thing, supposedly a treat, that turns out shitty when you actually get to try it. I need to be vertical, I think. I need to stand on my own two feet. I start up, get the spins, sit down. When everything subsides, I crawl—I crawl—across twenty feet of gravel on my hands and knees, over to the car and I drag myself upright and I lean against the hood, breathing like a drowning man.

In a minute, after thinking it over, Worm follows.

The sky, I think, remembering New Jersey. The low clouds lit by hepatitis lights. This could have all stopped there. I could have left him there the first time. Except I couldn't, as it turned out. I flat couldn't. Suddenly I'm angry, at Worm, at myself, I don't know. Just pissed. The waste of it.

"What were you fucking thinking in there?" I ask him. "I had those guys. I had 'em."

"I was trying to give you an edge," he says.

"Fuck you."

"I said I was sorry," he says. "I took my shot and I missed. It happens."

"It happens all the time around you, Worm."

"It happens to you, too, Mike," he says; suddenly wounded. "You're the one who took the big fall before I came out. You had about three fucking dollars in your pocket when I saw you."

"Fuck you," I tell him, stung by the memory. "That's different."

"No, fuck you," Worm says. "It's always different for you, isn't it? Your shot is somehow more noble, mine's not worth shit. You think you're the only one with ambitions."

"Yeah?" I ask him. "What's your ambition?"

It's a cruel question, I know it. That's what friends are for, to help each other preserve our illusions about ourselves. Worm's all right. That's his delusion, he thinks he's all right. Actually he's fucking broken.

"You know . . ." he says.

"No, I don't know," I say to him. "You fucking tell me."

I watch his face, running through the combinations, trying to find the answer. He isn't dumb. That's not the problem.

Finally he says, "I don't know. I don't think like that."

"You don't think, period."

I mean this to be cruel, and Worm sees this, and it registers. Things are being broken here. But he's still got his dignity.

"Exactly," he says. "I don't think. I just try and get by. That's the best I can do now. You weren't in there with me, Mike, you just don't know. The constant fucking noise and the banging and the yelling. You never sleep, you only wait till morning. It changes you. We're different now, Mike, you and me."

He pauses for a second, to let the story sink in, and I think: Bullshit. So I tell him, "Bullshit."

"You don't know, man," he says, hurt. "You weren't inside."

"I've known you since the second grade," I tell him. "You aren't a dime's worth of different than you were then. Spare me the prison movie, okay?"

Now he's pissed.

"You're so smart," he says. "You're looking down the road, always figuring, calculating the odds, playing your man. You're the one who thinks he's going pro. You see yourself in the fucking Mirage, don't you? Rubbing elbows with Johnny Chan. You think you can beat the game, straight up, don't you? Don't you?"

I don't say anything. So far he's right.

"But you can't," Worm says. "I know it can't be done. The only way is to have an edge. That's the one thing I know. That's my way."

That's it, I think. End of the road.

"Okay," I tell him. "What's our edge now? You tell me. We owe fifteen grand in a day. How do we play this, Ace?"

"This?" he says. "This you know. We fold the fucking hand. Get the fuck out of Dodge. There's plenty of places besides New York City where guys like us can earn a living. We'll be back on our feet in no time."

"Not me," I tell him.

"What do you mean?"

"I'm not living like that. What are you talking about? Baltimore? Detroit? Plus, you ever get big enough to show your head above the grass, Grama comes after you anyway. No thanks. I'm going to go back to the city. Talk to Grama, see if I can find somebody to stake me . . ."

Worm looks embarrassed again. He turns away, looking up into the sky: low, blank, vacant.

"It's not just Grama," he says.

"What are you talking about?" I ask him. "You said Grama was on his own."

"Yeah, but you didn't believe me, did you?"

I don't give him anything, waiting for the last little jigsaw piece to come tumbling out.

Worm says, "The truth is Teddy KGB bankrolled that cock-diesel psycho."

I ought to be more surprised than I am. Still this is bad news, the worst. There's nobody below KGB on the list of people I don't want to fuck with. I see his face, his mouth, his teeth black with cookie mush, and a little thrill of danger runs along my spine.

"You've fucked us in the ass this time, Worm," I says.

"You see what I mean," Worm says. "Highway time."

"I'm still not going."

"What the fuck?"

I spit a little puddle of blood out onto the gravel.

"I'd rather face it now," I tell him. "If they're going to do me worse than this, I want to see it coming. Besides, it's no fucking way to live, looking over your shoulder."

"You can drop me at the bus station, man."

"You do it your way," I tell him. "I'll do it mine."

"Okay, I'll walk to the fucking station," he says.

He stands there staring at me, looking at whatever kind of animal I've turned into, a thing he doesn't recognize, and I think: this is it. When he goes, he's gone.

"Later," Worm says.

He turns, and walks away, and I can tell—he's waiting for me to come with him, to follow him or fetch him back, to set him on his feet again and point him in the right direction, and for a second I think he is right. He doesn't have what he needs. I owe him that, to take care of him. But it's his life. He's going to have to learn how to live it someday, either that or die trying. I can't help him, either way. I know it and still I almost follow, almost go after him. I can tell he's waiting for me.

I don't go after him.

When he's far enough away to know this, he turns for one last shot.

"At least you're rounding again," he says. "One of these days you're going to thank me for that."

I don't say anything. He waits for me to say something but I don't. Then he hunches his shoulders into the leather jacket and he turns his back on me and walks away, down the sidewalk, around the corner, gone.

Alone in the parking lot. I look up into the night sky: nothing for me. Nothing and nobody. I was born alone, I tell myself. I dream alone and I'm going to die alone. It's cold comfort. In a minute I get back into the rent-a-car and I'm gone, myself.

fold or hang tough. Call or raise the bet. These are decisions you make at the table. Sometimes the odds are stacked so clear there's only one way to play it. Other times, like holding a small pair against two over cards, it's six to five or even money, either way. Then it's all about feel, what's in your guts.

I knock on the door to Grama's place and the same hostess looks out through the door. I can see her eyes widen when she sees my face. I cleaned up as best I could in the bathroom sink but I've been beaten, hard. You can tell. People on the subway, on the way over, they take one look at me and switch cars.

The Korean whore is still on the phone apparently. The same smell of spermicide and sweat. The hostess doesn't say a word, goes back to check with Grama and then he comes out to see for himself.

"Look at you," he says.

"Look at me," I tell him.

"You want to come in?"

"Nah."

"Where's your friend?"

"Gone," I tell him. It doesn't sit well.

"You better come in," he says, and this time it's not an invitation. It's an order.

I follow him down the dim hallway, into the mess of his office. The dogs are gone today. In their place are two more whores, doing each other's nails while they wait for clients. Grama closes the door behind me but he doesn't shoo the girls away, which I take to be a good sign. He leans against the desk.

"So you brought the money," he says.

"A little short," I tell him.

"How short?"

"The whole way."

His face twitches, pained.

"There must be some kind of story," he says.

"I don't figure you want to hear it."

"Your friend Worm."

"He's really gone," I tell him. "And you can see, you can see for yourself, I can't pay."

"You're banged up pretty good."

"I would if I could."

"You never should have vouched for that scumbag," Grama says. I shrug at him. Maybe he's right. I mean, definitely he's right. But it's a little late. Grama says, "You're leaving me no outs here."

"What do you mean?"

"I can't trust you two aren't playing me."

I turn this over in my head and he's right—I can't prove we're not.

"I'm not the one working with a partner," I tell him.

But this just pisses him off. "You want to take this up with KGB, go ahead. Otherwise, you've got a day."

"Come on," I tell him—but he cuts me off with a wave of his hand.

"The whole thing," Grama says. "Fifteen thousand. Tomorrow. That's the whole deal, best I can do for you. I don't have to tell you, if you miss it, you know. I really don't have any choice."

"I understand."

"It's what I do," he says. Then he goes over to the door and holds it open for me to go.

"I'll see you tomorrow," he says.

And then I'm out and out of the front hall and out into the street and I'm breathing the free air again and I'm about to cry, it feels so good. I check my watch: four o'clock. Eight hours to midnight, which is one version of "tomorrow," and thirty-two hours till tomorrow midnight. Sometime in there, my time is up. And me only fourteen thousand nine hundred dollars short. And the one thing I know, the one thing I can say for sure, is that I never want to be inside Grama's office again.

So: I draw a blank.

So maybe Worm was right. Time to play far, far away. I hadn't gotten a fucking thing off Grama, which I didn't really expect to. Worm was right about that much. But I thought I might get some little glimmer, a little flash of light somewhere. There is a way out of this, I told myself. I just didn't see it yet.

I start to move down the sidewalk, down toward Canal Street, moving with the other bodies, drifting along. I thought about how easy it would be to just disappear into the faces—not these faces, not unless I wanted to learn Chinese—but to just do the fade, the way Worm did. And, really, I'd still be alive, still be the person I am with the memories I've got and the skills. My folks are dead, my sister lives in Phoenix, which is the next-best thing to being dead. She sends me a card at Christmas and I send her one, usually the day after I get hers. How much smaller would her life be if I wasn't in it?

Five in the afternoon, the loneliest hour in the life of the city. Everybody's hurrying home, meeting friends, lighting the lights in their kitchens. Except for the ones who've been left out. We recognize each other on the street but we're polite enough to pretend not to. Sure you've got a wife, a home, a social life, and a sex life. Sure you're okay. Me, too.

What's keeping me? I wonder.

Why not just dive in, submerge myself in the millions of other faces? Grama would never find me, nor KGB, as long as I stayed out of the card rooms. All I'd have to do is switch names, find a way to make a living. And I know, like I say, this isn't the end of the world. End up as a parts salesman in Philadelphia and you'll find some way to like it. I don't see how but I know people do it. All I need to do is go home, pack my bags, touch somebody— maybe Knish, maybe even Jo—for a little getaway fund and then I'm on my way. All I've got to do is throw away the person I am, become nobody again.

I'm not quite ready to do it though.

Not that I have made a great success out of being Michael McDermott. Currently mutt of the world: ex-student, ex-boyfriend, maybe ex-human by this time tomorrow. People pass me on the street, they take one look at my face and they edge over to the other side of the sidewalk. I've got the marks of violence on me.

Soon to be a major motion picture, I think. As soon as Grama gets the green light from KGB.

I want to live, I think.

I want to live or die as myself. This seems like a foolish thought, a feeling, a sentiment. I mean, I could be somebody else. I could live in this body and have a completely different life than the one I've got now. But I'm attached to this life. I'm used to it. I've got the clothes for this weather. Also: there's no guarantee that I wouldn't fuck up this imaginary new life as bad as I've managed to fuck up this one I'm living. "Auto Parts Clerk in Rampage," I think. "Ideal Husband Goes Berserk."

This still doesn't help though. I still don't see any outs. Odds are good that, this time tomorrow, I'll be riding the dog out of here anyway. If I live that long.

I still can't think of anything—nothing good anyway. Maybe I could tap the money off of Knish but I wouldn't want to do that. Even if he had it.

After a while, though, any idea starts to sound good if you aren't having any other ideas. I dip into a nasty dark bar and find a pay phone, dial the Chesterfield. When Petra answers, it's like a voice from some other time, some better time.

"Hey, Mikey," she says, putting as much sex into it as usual. "We going to see you around here? You're playing everyplace but our place, I hear."

"I'll be around," I tell her, trying to keep my voice cool. I wonder what she'd think if she saw my face right now. I tell her, "Hey, I'm looking for Knish."

"He was here a while ago," she says. "I'll check." A minute later she comes back on the line. "He took off a while ago. Zagosh said he thought he was going to go take some steam. You want to leave a message for him? He'll be back."

"That's okay," I tell her. "I'll find him. Thanks."

"Are you fucking up, Mike?" Petra asks. "I hear stories."

"I'll tell you later," I say; ease the phone down into the cradle again and leave. It's good to have a sense of purpose again, a mission, even if it's not much of one: the Russian baths on Twenty-third Street. I wonder what kind of stories. All it would take is one look at my face but still, somebody knows something, probably more than I do. Somebody's been talking. That feeling where everybody in the world knows what's going on, everybody but you. Some important piece of information that you don't know.

The baths: white tile, bright lights, gigantic Russian guys like fire hydrants draped in towels. The chest hair itself is amazing on these old guys, white hair so thick it looks like a bath mat. I find Knish where I expect to: some tile-lined room at about a hundred and sixty degrees. I'm sweating my ass off in my street clothes but Knish looks right at home in a towel.

"You look like Duane Bobick after the first round with Norton," he says, looking at my face. This is what people do lately when they see me. "What the fuck happened to you?"

"Worm," I tell him.

"That motherfucker," Knish says. "When are you going to listen?"

"I'm listening."

"Cops get involved?"

"You could say that," I tell him. "Look, I got my pockets emptied."

"Worm did that to you?"

"No, it was a series of—I don't know. One fuckup after another. Mine was going along with him."

"Talk to me," Knish says. "What do you need? Five hundred, a grand?"

For a second I don't think I'm going to tell him. I don't see how I can. But then the silence goes on too long, and I see that I've got to. Too late to stop now.

"I need fifteen thousand dollars," I tell him.

He goes through a series of expressions while he reacts to this: disbelief, concern, finally anger. He's pissed.

"Fifteen?" he asks. "You need fifteen thousand. Yeah, and I need a blow job from Christy Turlington. Get the fuck out of here."

"Seriously," I tell him, and his black eyes focus down on me. "Joey, what can you do for me? Five hundred isn't even going to get me started."

I can hear in my own ears how pathetic I sound, and I wonder how I let myself get this far. Knish hears it, too.

"Goddamnit, Mike," he says. "If five hundred won't help, what's two grand going to do? What kind of trouble are you in anyway?"

"The worst kind," I tell him. "With the worst guy."

"KGB," he says.

I don't say anything. I don't have anything much to say.

Knish says, "Didn't I tell you never let these guys get a hold of you?"

"You told me a lot of things."

"Yeah, and you didn't listen," he says. Now he's getting warmed up. He paces back and forth across the tile floor in his towel, worrying at me like a little dog. "I tell you to play within your means, you risk your whole bankroll. I tell you not to overextend yourself—to rebuild—you go into hock for more. I was giving you a living, Mike, showing you the playbook I put together off my own beats. But that wasn't enough for you."

No, it wasn't, I think. But now is not the time to say it. Suddenly I just want to have this be over, get the fuck out of there.

"Look, Knish," I tell him. "Now is not the time to tell me how bad I fucked up. I know I fucked up. Every part of me hurts. What I need this time is whatever money you can give me."

"That's what I'm trying to tell you," Knish says. "This time there is no money."

This hits me like a body shot, square in the gut. This was the last thing I expected.

"I give you two grand, what's that buy you?" he asks. "A day? A week? No, I give it to you, I'm wasting it."

"That's fucking great," I tell him.

"You did it to yourself," Knish says. He looks at me, cool. It isn't that he doesn't like me, or that he doesn't care. There just isn't any way around it he can see.

He says, "You had to put it all on the line for some Vegas pipe dream."

Which pisses me off. "Sure, Knish, I took some risks," I tell him. "You? You see all the fucking angles, but you never have the stones to play one."

"Stones?" he says, irate. "Stones, you little punk? I'm not playing for the fucking thrill of victory here. What am I, eighteen years old? I owe rent, alimony, child support. I play for money. My kids eat. I have stones enough not to chase cards, action, or fucking pipe dreams of winning the World Series on ESPN. Asshole."

"Okay," I tell him. "I'll see you."

But he isn't done yet.

"Let me tell you how it works," he says. "I'm twenty years old, right? And I'm a basketball player, third-team All-America in the *Sporting News*, captain of the team. I bet you didn't know that about me, did you? Then one day I'm going after a ball out of bounds and I trip over a folding chair and then I can't move my knee after that. Take a look."

He holds his leg up toward me, a pale thin hairy monkey leg, to show the double zipper-line scar of an old-fashioned knee surgery.

"So the coach cuts me, next day," Knish says. "How's that for a bad beat? Doesn't even wait around. Just like that, he loosed the dead weight."

"Meaning me," I say. "Now it's you loosing the dead weight."

"That's the way the fucking world works," he says. "You don't like it, maybe you can find a better one someplace. But don't pretend it isn't like that. Look, Mike—" and here his voice softens, he's almost pleading— "all the degenerates in this town, you're the one I can talk to. The only one I see myself in. You want me to call some people, try and get you some time, I will. Place to stay, or the truck, no problem. But about the money, I've got to do this. I've got to say no."

"Fine," I tell him. "I understand. I'll see you."

I walk away without shaking his hand. I don't mind about the money, or maybe I do, I don't know—but it's this fucking judgment that bothers me. He's right, I'm wrong. Another fucking rabbi. I'm sick of it is all.

"Maybe that's the way *your* world works," I tell him, turning.

I catch him staring after me, sorrowful.

"What?" he says.

"I *did* put it all on the line," I tell him. "It's true. And you know what? It wasn't a bad beat. I wasn't unlucky. I was outplayed that time. But I know I'm good enough to sit at that table. It's not a fucking pipe dream, Knish. I'm not chasing rainbows. I know all about obligations."

"The hell you do," Knish says.

"I know about *your* obligations anyway. God knows I hear about them enough. And I'm not saying you're wrong to do what you do, I understand it, it makes sense to me. But there's more for me than just getting by."

Knish is getting that sad look again.

He tells me, "I don't doubt your talent . . ."

"Listen," I tell him, quick, before he can let me know what a stupid loser I am. "Listen, I never told anybody this. One night, seven, eight months ago, real late at the Taj, I see Johnny Chan walk in and sit three hundred-six hundred bucks. The room just stops. Everybody puts an eye on him, and he's just beating up the table. Forty-five minutes of this and the craps tables are dead. All the high rollers are in watching, and some are playing with him. They're fucking giving away their money to him so they can say they played with the two-time World Champion. So you know what I did?"

"I don't want to know," Knish says.

"I sat down at the table."

"You'd need fifty, sixty grand to play right in that game."

"I had six. But I wanted to know."

"And what did you find out?"

"I played tight for an hour, mostly folded. Tight as the pope's asshole. But then I made a score."

"Aces, right?" Knish says. "Or kings."

"Rags," I tell him. "Fucking nothing. And Chan raises. But I decide, just decide, that I'm going to forget about the money and fucking out-play him this hand. Because I think he's got nothing. Re-raise."

"You played right back at him."

"And then he comes right back over the top at me," I tell him. "Trying to bull me like all those tourists he's been beating. I hesitate for like two seconds and then re-raise. Chan looks at me.

Makes a move toward his checks, looks back at his cards, one more time at me . . . then he throws his hand in the muck."

"You took it down," Knish says.

" 'You have it?' he asks me. 'Sorry, John, I don't remember,' I tell him. I get up and walk straight to the cashier. I sat with the best in the world, and I won."

"You put a fucking move on Chan, and you won," Knish says, in a kind of wonder. "So that's why you made the run at that no-limit game."

"That's right," I tell him. "And I'll do it again if I live long enough."

This time when he looks up, there's a kind of respect in his eyes. That's all I wanted.

"Then I'm rooting for you, Mike," he says; reaches his hand out and we shake hands and we're done. But I've got a little of what I came for.

A little, not a lot. Back on the street, it's almost dark and I'm still short the whole way, and tomorrow's coming. And now, with Knish out, I'm running out of ideas. I drift down into the subway down into the station with the others. Everybody's on their way somewhere. Going home, making dates, selling crack to kinder-gartners, I don't know. I wait with all the others and this is what I think: I'm the free one. I could just come dislocated tomorrow, drift out all the way. All the rest of them are anchored into their lives, they are who they are, they're going to stay that way. The cop on the corner and the bills and the paperboy and the wives and the kids and the elevator girl at the office, the one who says hi in the morning—all these people are just caught in this web of connections, like Gulliver, the thousand tiny strands that hold you down. While I've busted them all, one by one, on purpose or not. One solid wind could blow me right away. It's a scary feeling but it's also not bad, not all the way. I feel like I own myself in a way that nobody else here does. Whatever I want to do. I just blink my eyes . . .

Uptown and over to the apartment but there is certainly nothing in the apartment for me. I look in the bathroom mirror and my clothes are okay and I'm as clean as I can be but the face is a wreck. If I am going to find a way out, it's not going to be here.

There's noplace else to go, either.

This is where I hit rock. This is the rock: I've got no money, no way to get the money, no rich aunts, no time to win the money, and no stake to start me with. I even think about Jo for a while but Jo doesn't have the money herself. And would her dad get off his Lexus butt and write a check for an ex-boyfriend, even if she asked him to? She could sell the car maybe, but not by tomorrow. And she wouldn't do it besides. I wouldn't do it if I were her.

Which leaves: nothing I can think of.

I sit there at the kitchen table while the clock in the stove turns over toward midnight. The poker books, the dreams of glory, look down at me from the shelves in the hall: Sklansky, Malmuth, Loomis, Brunson. These were going to be my friends, my equals. And I do remember that look of respect in Knish's eyes and it does make me feel all right—right up to the moment where I remember that I have played this like a fool. I could have stayed out of the no-limit game with KGB. I could have prepared for moot court. I could have let Worm lead his own life, right from the start. He's no better off now than he was and I am much, much worse. I could have played the kings, in Binghamton.

Apparently I didn't do any of those things.

I remember the fucking rabbi look on Knish's face, he's-right-I'm-wrong. I hate that judgment look—the look on Marinacci's face when I was fucking the dog at moot court, the drink and judgment with Petrovsky. Everybody's right but me. Everybody knows.

But Petrovsky. . . . It's the one number I haven't dialed. He's the one who told me, after all: You can only care about what you care about.

Maybe he will, I think. Probably he won't. I won't die of embarrassment if he turns me down. Still something in me doesn't want to, doesn't want to invite the judgment. I don't want to know what my life looks like to him. I think of my own father, somewhere, dead. I think about what he would say.

I don't want to, after I think for a second. I don't want to at all.

But I sit there thinking for another hour, and no other names show up, no other outs. If this is the best you got, I tell myself, you are in worse shape than I thought. But it's not the best shot, it's the only shot, from where I sit. I make my way back uptown again, back toward the law school, the familiar streets at night, the places I walked with Jo, talking about the things we were going to do and the places we were going to go. All of that seems like a lie to me, a bright shiny thing that a kid might pick up off the street. Petrovsky knows this: you can only care about what you care about. People do it. People lie to themselves and turn themselves into something they're not, live lives they don't care about. It hollows them out inside. I know. That was my house, growing up. A line from a Bob Dylan song keeps circling around and around in my head: to live outside the law you must be honest . . .

No more bullshit, I tell myself. After this—if there is anything after this—no more pretending, no more lying to myself, no more fakery. You must be honest. Actually, I have no fucking idea what this means or how you might go about it but it sounds like a good idea. It might keep me out of trouble.

Petrovsky's light is on when I go by, good. I hesitate for a minute, though it's way too late to back out. I really don't want to do this. I really don't see any other choice.

I ride the elevator up to his floor. The hallways are clean and empty and smell of floor wax and I still don't feel like doing this. It's embarrassing, for one thing. It's opening a side of me that Petrovsky doesn't want to know about, and I don't want him to see. But still . . . I can feel my world narrowing, things getting cut off, moving faster, and part of me just wants to get the thing over with, get to the showdown. Whatever happens, happens.

I knock on the door and hear his voice inside, old, tired, telling me to come in.

"Hello, Professor," I tell him, walking up into the light. There's just the lamp on his desk, books and papers walled around him. He's been working. His eyes narrow when he sees my face, and I watch him working the combinations as I pull up his visitor's chair and sit. He doesn't know how to play it, the face.

"Are you in pain, Michael?" he asks.

"It's not that bad," I tell him.

"It looks very bad," he says. "Have you seen a doctor?"

"No. I don't need to really."

He disapproves. He has to: he has to stand for something, he has to stand for what is right. At the same time, he is not without mercy. Which is why I am here.

He says, "There's something else you need perhaps?"

I don't answer, not yet. I let the question hang in the air while he opens his desk drawer and gets out the office bottle, gin, and pours himself a coffee cup and pours one for me and slides it across the desk.

"Thanks," I tell him. But I don't touch it. I'm on a mission here.

"Should I consider you withdrawn from school?" he asks.

"I guess so."

"Is this temporary or permanent?"

"You know," I tell him. "You told me yourself—I'm no lawyer."

This seems to startle him—maybe I played it a little too hard—but it's the truth and we both know it. He takes a nice long swallow of raw gin while he thinks about it. It doesn't take any of the shine out of his eyes. Not yet. It will by midnight.

"I hope my little story didn't discourage you," he says.

"Not at all," I tell him. "Not at all. It was what I needed to hear. I was already on my way."

"But now you're here," he says, and turns the headlights on me, looking at my face, my eyes, my hands. The rabbi of the law, he can see under the skin, into the mind and the heart. He has a law, he knows right from wrong. But he is not without mercy.

"Are you in trouble?" he asks gently.

"Yes, I am."

He makes a question with his face.

"Not with the law," I tell him. "I owe."

"A gambling debt?"

"Not mine," I tell him. "I vouched for the wrong guy, and now it's on me."

Petrovsky settles back into his chair, cradling his cup with both hands, and for the few seconds while he thinks, I disappear, the office disappears, nothing but the beautiful machinery of his mind. I can practically hear it, whirring and racing, the tiny gears meshing.

"Perhaps I can use my contacts," he finally says, leaning forward again. "I have a few. Maybe I can make this go away for you."

My turn to think. It's not a bad idea, on the face of it—Petrovsky's poker game could sew up anybody they wanted to. On the other hand, I'd never get a game in this town again, or any other town, not when the word got out. It's the same devil's bargain as running away: lose your life to save your life.

He's waiting for an answer.

"I appreciate that, Professor, I really do," I finally tell him. "But, you know, living in this world, I can't do it that way."

"I understand," he says. "So, what will it take for you to be free of this?"

"I need fifteen thousand," I tell him. "Tonight."

"So much?" he asks me, genuinely shocked. "Michael, so much? I'm not a wealthy man."

"I know. It kills me to ask. But it's the only play I have."

I sit there under the light while he searches my face, looking for any sign of falsity, any hustle at all. He is kind but he is not stupid. I need to show him that I am genuine; and so, although it hurts me to do it, I let him know how badly I need it.

"Can you help me, Professor?" I ask him, as quietly and sincerely as I can muster. "Anything at all," I say.

Oh, this hurts: to know that I have given this my best, that I have taken my chances and gone where I had to and still come up so far short that I am dependent on his mercy. It hurts to know this. It hurts worse to show it, but there is no other way. I watch him figuring, calculating. This is my life, I think, this right here. Please don't give me justice, I think. I don't want what I deserve. I want a chance, an opportunity.

"I hate seeing you like this, Michael," he finally says. And I see that he is going to turn me down, and my heart knots up in my chest and starts to burn, noxious, like a burning plastic bag. "I want to help you. But fifteen thousand dollars . . ."

"I understand," I tell him.

"Fifteen thousand dollars," he says again. "If it must be tonight, then ten is the best I can do."

I shake my head, to make sure that I heard him right, but I did hear him right and I have a chance. It's not everything, not at all, but it's that one little glimmer of light, the one I've been waiting for.

"Would you do that?" I ask him. "Would you do that for me?"

He looks at me, one last testing glare, and then he slowly nods.

He has a lesson for me, too. He leans toward me. "When my mother let me leave the yeshiva," he says, "it almost broke her. But she knew the life I had to lead. To do that for another is a mitzvah, and for that I owe. So take this money and get yourself out of this trouble, Michael. I know you can do it."

He pauses for a second, to let this sink in, then digs a checkbook out of his desk drawer. I watch him like a hungry dog, slowly unscrewing his fountain pen, carefully writing the numbers in a fine old-fashioned handwriting like my grandmother's. Before he signs, he looks up one last time, into my face. He wants to make sure he isn't making a mistake. Then he signs, rips the check out, and hands it to me.

"I promise—" I start in.

But he cuts me off with a wave of his hand.

"No promises," he says. "You'll do your best, I'm sure. Now listen—there's an all-night check-cashing place on Forty-seventh and Tenth, northeast corner. Speak to Moishe there, he'll cash my check, no questions."

"Thank you," I tell him.

"No," he says quickly. "You can thank me with your life, your actions. Good luck."

He waves his hand in my direction, a final blessing, and I am dismissed. I fold the check into my shirt pocket and I can feel it burning there, all the way downstairs, all the way crosstown to Moishe's check-cashing place. It's maybe eleven o'clock, maybe a little after. The clouds are racing between the buildings in a broken sky. I'm a man again, it feels like. One little piece of paper. But I don't feel broken anymore, I feel like I've got a little headway going here. I'll either make it or I'll go down standing. That's all I ask.

But Moishe doesn't like my looks, not one bit. I don't like them much myself, not after last night, but there's nothing I can do about it. He stares at me through the bulletproof glass, back at the check, back at my face and for a second I think he's just going to rip it up. Instead he goes over to the telephone and dials the number off the check. No answer. What if this doesn't work? But it has to work. I've got one night, tonight. I've got one chance and it's this one.

Moishe goes to his Rolodex, next, and I wonder—while he slowly, carefully dials the phone—what business Petrovsky would have with this guy so he should have his number in the office. Family business, is my guess—but maybe there's a shady side to the professor, too. It makes me feel better to think so. I wait while Moishe talks. After he hangs up, he still doesn't like it. But he gets the money anyway, and counts it out for me in the metal tray under the window: stacks of hundred-dollar bills, one thousand, two thousand, three . . . I take the money and I pile it together and snap a rubber band around it. When I put it in my pocket, it makes a nice big bulge. Here we go, I think. Quick, before I can stop and think about it any longer, I head off to the last stop, the only place there is to go for me, to Teddy KGB's.

i've seen them at the tables before, all the time, the lost ones. Short-stacked and long odds against, all their outs gone, with only one last card in the deck that can help them. I used to wonder how they could let themselves get into such bad shape. I thought it showed a lack of self-respect to show themselves in public like that. I thought it was their fault, that there was something wrong with them, something they needed that they didn't have. Now I know better. One chance, long odds, no tomorrow.

Walking into Teddy's place I feel like Buckner walking back into Shea Stadium. The smell, the gray walls, the Russian meat in their indestructible polyester all make me seasick. Then Teddy is standing there in front of me. He's smiling, and I know that smile. I remember that smile.

"So you have my money?" Teddy says.

"I owe you that money tomorrow, right?"

"*Da*."

"So until then it's mine?"

Teddy shrugs.

"For the next eight hours it's yours," he says. "But if you don't have it all by then, then *you* are mine."

"If it's like that," I tell him, "I've got ten grand, and I'm looking for a game."

"What?"

"You heard me."

"You learned nothing from that last lesson I taught you."

"I learned plenty," I tell him.

He starts to think. He takes one of his fucking cookies out of the bag, unscrews it, and holds it up by his ear, like he's listening to it. Then he absently slips the Oreo into his mouth. Then he comes to his decision.

"So we'll play," he says. "Heads up. We both start with a couple of racks. Blinds twenty-five and fifty. We play till one of us has it all."

"Freeze-out, yeah? It's your game, it's your place—it's a sucker play."

He doesn't budge, just stares at me with those junky eyes of his, slow-moving, glassy, unreadable. He's good, I know that already.

"Let's do it," I tell him.

"Good," he says.

Ten minutes later we are sitting in one of the back rooms of Teddy's place with ten thousand in chips in front of each of us and a circle of railbirds all around, watching. Heads-up games, one man on one man, always turn into dogfights. Freeze-out is worse, and with this kind of money on the table somebody's going to get hurt. That's what they came to watch. It's like the fucking car races—nobody comes to watch the cars drive around in a little circle a hundred times. They come for the crashes. That's what the railbirds are waiting for, the sight of blood, and nobody thinks it's going to be Teddy's. Nobody but me.

Teddy deals the first hand: king of hearts, king of diamonds in the hole. God does love me, yes He does. He shows His bounty in the form of wired kings.

"Raise, Teddy," I tell him. "A thousand straight."

He laughs at me.

"Very aggressive," he says. "It's a new day and you won't be pushed around. But I re-raise. Five thousand."

Here we go, I think. A little early in the night for this. The key to no-limit poker is to put your man to a decision for all his chips, that's what Brunson says. And that's what Teddy has just done to me. He's representing aces, the only hand better than my cowboys. I can't call—that gives him five more cards to catch a hand. No, I've got two ways and two ways only to play this hand: either I believe him, and I fold. Either that or I go all in. I watch his face but nothing in it moves. There's no light in his eyes at all. There's nothing in that face to help me. He doesn't fidget, he doesn't move. Which leaves me—what?

Which leaves me mathematics anyway. That and the laws of probability. They're on my side. He doesn't have any fucking aces, or at least he doesn't have two of them.

"Re-raise," I tell him. "All in."

I shove the stack of checks toward the center of the table, leaving me empty, no outs. I watch Teddy. He takes an Oreo out, unscrews the top, looks in the middle—to see if there's a million dollars there, I guess, or a crystal ball—then folds.

"Take it down," he says. He was trying to buy it.

Okay, I think, raking the pot in. Okay okay okay. This is very good. See, in heads-up play, the size of your stack is almost as important as the cards. I chopped one of Teddy's legs out from under him in the very first hand: my original thousand bet plus his five thousand raise plus the big blinds mean he's lost way over half of his ten thousand before I can even get a cigarette in my mouth. Now all I have to do is lean on him until he falls over.

No hurry, I tell myself. We've got all night.

I stick a cigarette in the corner of my mouth and I don't light this one, studying Teddy all the while for his tells, the little twitch or wiggle that will give the hand away. I play the next few hands tight, folding a lot of hands that I'd bet in other company. I don't want to open myself up. Thing is, in a heads-up game with good-size blind bets, you can get eaten up just with the blinds playing passive. So: I'm waiting for the hand, watching and waiting. Teddy still isn't giving anything away. It's in there somewhere, I think.

Maybe I won't need it.

An hour into the game I come up with jacks in the hole. Not quite enough, I think, but maybe . . . I raise and re-raise before the flop, building the pot. Teddy sticks right with me. The flop comes: no help. I try to think of some hand Teddy might be working on but there's pretty much nothing, a pair of sixes showing.

Then the turn comes: jack of diamonds, my old friend. That puts me full, jacks over sixes. I lay low, minimum bet, watch Teddy call. He's sitting on trips, three sixes, is what I think. That's a hand that's good enough to win, most of the time. I wait for that last card—praying to Jesus, anybody, let it be anything but a six—and the seven of clubs falls and this hand is mine.

"Tap," I tell Teddy. "I bet your stack."

He looks at me, lazy, appraising. Then he grins, his black teeth full of cookie mush.

"Okay," he says. "Call."

"Jacks up," I tell him, turning the pair.

"They're good," he says, shrugs his shoulders, mucks his hand, pushes himself away from the table, and stands up, stretching. I start to stack the checks in front of me but there's no mystery: I've got my ten thousand and his ten thousand. I can pay Grama off and I'm still halfway to Petrovsky. A nice hour's work.

"So, that's it then," Teddy says, hovering. "Just like a young guy, coming in here for a quickie. I feel so unsatisfied."

"I'm really sorry," I tell him.

"You must feel proud and good. Strong enough to beat the world."

"I feel fine."

"Me, too," says Teddy KGB. "I feel okay."

"Good," I tell him. "I'll just cash out then. Pay you your money and leave."

I stand up then, dig my jacket up and start to put it on. There's something going on, though, something in the air. All my little antennae are picking it up.

"Maybe we should check with one other guy," Teddy says. "See how he feels."

"Who's that?"

Teddy doesn't answer me, just turns and yells over his shoulder, down the hallway into the darkness beyond: "Grama!"

In a second—just quick enough to let me know he's been watching, waiting—Grama comes shambling into the room. He's still wearing his hat.

"I thought I smelled him," I say to KGB.

"I'll take what's ours," Grama says to me.

He's pissed. Though I don't know why—he gets his money, nobody gets beat up, it's like a happy ending in a fairy tale. But no doubt he's pissed. He looks at me with his little pig eyes and he looks like he might just beat the crap out of me anyway, just for the pleasure of the thing. I carefully cut out three racks of chips, three-quarters of the total, and slide them across the table to him.

"Of course you could let it ride," Teddy says to me. "Take your chances. You'll let that happen, won't you, Grama?"

Grama looks confused for a second. He isn't sure what Teddy wants him to say. Then makes up his mind, or whatever it is in there.

"Sure, partner," he says. "He's still got till morning to make good."

"No, thanks," I tell them. Just looking at Grama makes me glad to be alive. Get me out of here, up on the street again and out of this stale air and far the fuck away from both of them, and I'll sing like Julie Andrews. I tell Teddy, "I'll just keep the five left over."

"Fine," Teddy says, and now he's pissed. "This is a fucking joke anyway. After all, I'm paying you with your own money."

"Meaning what?"

"Your money," Teddy says. "I'm still up twenty grand from the last time I stuck it in you."

Grama laughs. The railbirds, the extras, KGB's hired meat all laugh along with the boss, a few jokes in Latvian or some shit. And I know what they're trying to do: they're trying to goad me into playing. Teddy doesn't like it when money leaves the room. But this isn't a gunfight and this isn't the OK Corral. It's not about pride or ego, it's just about money. I think it over. I can walk now, even with the bulletheads and halfway back to paying Petrovsky, a nice safe play.

The other thing is, I was wrong when I told Jo that the money was just a way of keeping score. Not this money. Not the money I'm playing with tonight. This is life and death, my life, my death. This is real. You can't lose what you don't put in the middle.

On the other hand, you can't win, either. This is what I came for, this is the feeling I want: one night, one table, one game. Everything comes down to what happens here. And I look at Teddy KGB and I'm up ten thousand already and I can take him. Even if I lose, I'm going to go down standing.

I pull the racks of chips back from Grama. "Deal 'em," I tell Teddy.

He springs to life immediately, before I can change my mind.

"Checks!" he yells, and one of the Russians hurries in from the next room with four new racks of chips.

"Double the blinds?" I ask him.

"Sure," he says, "Table stakes."

"Feel free to re-load at any time," I tell him.

Which pisses him off, of course, but I like him pissed off. Anything to get him off-balance. That first ten thousand has got to be bothering him—not that he can't spare it, or ten times it, but he doesn't seem like a person who likes to lose. Especially not in front of the polyester boys, not in front of Grama, not in his own damn club.

So Teddy goes on a tear. He bets on threes, he bets on aces, he raises and re-raises on a pair of fours. He plays like a fucking maniac—which will be his downfall in the long run, if I can hold on long enough, but that is the question. It's not even a strategy unless it works. But he catches a few hands, he squeezes me out of a couple of others, on one hand he catches a fourth seven on the fucking river, me sitting on an ace-high club flush, and nails me hard on it. I haven't found his tell yet, assuming he's got one, and this mad-dog style of his is driving me nuts. I'm just waiting, waiting for the tide to turn. The question is whether I'll have any money left when it does.

Twenty turns into ten turns into five thousand and Teddy's got a magic fucking kingdom stacked up in front of him, towers and cities of checks.

I've got five thousand left. This money is real tonight. It's not just play.

Ace of hearts, five of diamonds in the hole. The flop comes down: ace of clubs, three of diamonds, five of spades. Two pair, aces and fives. I look at Teddy's hand: nothing in sight, nothing but the straight. And Teddy re-raised before the flop. For him to have the straight, he would have had to re-raise holding a two and a four. Even in his mad-dog phase, Teddy wouldn't do that. Unless he just did. But Teddy doesn't have the straight. I'm going to win this hand.

"You must be kicking yourself," Teddy says. "You could have walked out way ahead. Bad judgment."

I look at his face, trying to read him: what's he got? Why's he trying to work me like this?

"Don't you worry, son," he says. "It'll all be over soon. Bet's to you."

I cut out half the stack I've got left, twenty-five hundred, ready to take him down. I pause for a second before I go in. I just want to read the air. Teddy looks anywhere, nowhere. He takes an Oreo absently from the cellophane and he unscrews it and he holds it up next to his ear for a second, like he was listening to it. He doesn't look at it. He listens to it. I have seen him do this before. When?

When I told him I was in, is when. When I told him I had come to play.

"I'm going to check," I tell him, pushing the chips back.

"No check here," Teddy says. "I tap you."

He counts my checks from across the table and pushes in a big bet, every penny I've got left. But it's too late.

I fold the hand, flip the hole cards up where he can see them.

"I'm going to lay these down," I tell him. "Big fucking cards. Top two. Because I know you played two-four, and I'm not drawing against a made hand."

This works just fine. He rakes the pot in, nothing on his face, but he's not crowing anymore. I can tell I got to him. He's trying to think. You get your opponent thinking, you're three-quarters of the way there.

"He lays down a monster," Teddy says. Supposedly he's talking to Grama but really he's trying to work it out for himself. "He should have paid me off on that . . ."

He turns to me, and now his eyes are alive and shiny.

"Why the fuck did you lay that down?" he asks.

I'm not saying anything.

He looks at his stacks, his hands. He smooths his clothes, trying out the gesture to see if he's used it. He's thinking. He knows it's something. Then, automatically, his hand dips down toward the cookies and he stops himself and he stares at his own hand like he wants to cut it off. He's found the traitor. In one quick movement he snatches the cookie package off the table and slams it into the far wall, where it explodes into crumbs.

"Not hungry, Teddy?" I ask him.

"Son of a bitch," he says, meaning, I think, me. "Let's play some cards."

I'll give him this: most guys would have gone on listening to the cookie until they were dead broke. Teddy spots his own tell after only one hand, he's that good. But no one's immune to getting a little rattled. I like him like this.

Plus his rattlesnake-with-a-hangover strategy only works when the cards cooperate. He keeps on playing aggressive but I get the hands to keep up. This bugs him, too—the little things that were working an hour ago are dying on him now. Plus everybody in his world is watching. There's no noise coming from anyplace else in the club, which means the other games are shut down. Everybody's hanging on the rail around us: this one table, this one night, under the light. I recognize a fringe of faces around the edges—Irving, Kenny, Grama—but I don't have time enough to spare for the crowd. I've got a game to play.

An hour later I'm back. I've got thirty on the table in front of me. Teddy sent one of his boys out front for more checks, just like I told him he would. Now he's got about thirty himself.

Grama leans over the rail as Teddy makes the cards. He says, "Quit fucking around, Teddy. Finish it."

"Hanging around, hanging around," Teddy says, playing to the crowd. "The kid's got alligator blood. I can't get rid of him."

Playing to the crowd, I think. That's just where I want him. KGB has got one weakness: he likes that dramatic gesture, the grand finale. He likes an audience. I can use this.

Blinds in.

Teddy deals me eight of spades, nine of spades. The two-flush keeps me in to the flop, as long as it stays cheap, which it does. The flop comes: six of diamonds, seven of spades, ten of hearts.

"Local Boy Makes Good."

The nut straight. I'm off to the fucking Mirage again, if I can play this right, which is how? But I know. I was born knowing.

"Check it," I tell Teddy.

"Two grand," he says. He flicks his chips in, a little carelessly, a little too casual. Something's up with him. Or maybe he suspects.

"Call the two thousand," I tell him, "and don't splash the pot."

"You're on a draw, Mike?" he says. "Go away, this one's no good for you. And in my club, I'll splash the pot whenever the fuck I please."

Still treating me like a kid. Fine with me. I watch him burn a card and then the turn: two of clubs.

"Okay, okay," I say. "Still checking to the boss."

Teddy says, "That's right. Big Poppa bets the pot."

He pushes forty-four hundred dollars in checks into the middle of the table. It's my turn to look worried. I think back, right to the start, back to that first no-limit game with Teddy, and I remember that liquid nitrogen floating around inside me. I remember his smile as he raked in the chips, and the gutshot feeling of sitting there afterward, and then I can feel the fear for real: what if he's really got it? What if he's got me this time again?

I feel this fear and I treasure it and I let a little show on my face as I cut out the checks and push them slowly, reluctantly, into the center. The only lie that's worth a shit is the one you tell yourself.

"I've got to call," I tell him, trying to keep up my front. "Otherwise I won't respect myself in the morning."

"Respect is all you'll have left in the morning," Teddy says, to a general little buzz of laughter and approval from his fans. Still playing to the house.

"Last card coming," he says.

The river comes: the ace of spades.

"Check," I tell him. I won't meet his eyes.

"It hurts, doesn't it?" Teddy asks. "You can't believe what fell. All your dreams dashed. Your hopes down the fucking drain. Grama standing right behind me, waiting."

He's watching me, tight. I look at his face and I remember him smiling, victorious, and I remember that I was just as sure *then* that I had him beat as I am now. And I think: this is a terrible mistake. And I let a little of this feeling onto my face, just a little. I don't know if he sees it or not.

Then he makes up his mind, all at once, and pushes in everything he has, every chip on the table in front of him, every nickel, all-in.

"That ace couldn't have helped you," he says. "I bet it all."

"You're right," I tell him. "It didn't help me."

I push the checks in, everything, every dollar on the table in one pot, and I flip my hole cards.

"I flopped the nut straight," I tell him, just for the pleasure of saying it.

"Motherfucker," Teddy says, mucking his hand and swatting his empty racks off the table, all in one gesture. Then turns to me.

"Motherfucker," he says in my face, and this time he means me. "That's it."

"That's it?" Grama says. "What the fuck do you mean, that's it? Take him down, Teddy."

But Teddy shakes his head. He's beaten.

"No more," he says. "Not this time. Son of a bitch checked it all the way," he says slowly, dreamily, like he still can't believe it. "Trapped me."

"You feeling satisfied now, Teddy?" I ask him. "Because I could go on busting you up all night."

This wakes him up: his eyes are glittering again, and Grama and the bodyguards are all tense. They can do me if they want to. They've got the beef. But I know my man.

Teddy slumps back down into his chair and says, "He beat me, straight up. Pay him. Pay the man his money."

And that's all. As big as he looked when I came in, that's how small he looks now. The room empties quickly as I stack the checks—nobody wants to see him like this. He's still there when I go to cash out, still sitting in his same chair, staring off into the distance on the other side of the table, trying to figure out where it went wrong on him; and in that moment, just for a second, I know what he is feeling and I think that nobody, nobody should have to feel like that.

all this is years ago by now, and a long ways away.

The person that I was then, I don't understand him anymore. I was still a kid at the age of thirty. That bothers me. That business of feeling sorry for KGB, that's a kid thing to do. I have these arguments with the person I used to be: Look, you want to win but you don't want anybody else to lose. Good luck with that one. You want part of the thing but not the whole thing. I'm not like that anymore: I want to win and I know it and I don't mind if the other guy has to eat his peck of shit that day. I've had my days. Maybe it's his turn.

I've got some money now, most likely more money than you. I've got the respect of the people that know me. I've got a house in Vegas and a condo in Ventura, right on the beach, where all the surfers go. You can watch them off the balcony. Last year I had a skin cancer taken off my forehead, from too much sun. I'm okay, just a little divot. It didn't spread. But still, for me to have that much sun, that felt like something. All that time at pools and patios and outside restaurants. I felt like I had figured something out, about how to live. New York seems like a nightmare to me now. I don't go back.

None of these people—not one of them—have I ever seen again in my life; although I still expect Worm to show up one of these days with a new story and a new scam. Petrovsky had a heart attack, a year after I left. Teddy KGB disappeared one day, end of story. Somebody knows, not me. Jo married a suit at a country club outside of Washington, D.C. His name sounded like money. I got an invitation but I understood that it was just a nice gesture. I wasn't meant to come.

And I am okay now, and I am even happy. I got married, it didn't take, but we still talk to each other. And lately, the last year or two, I've been going out with Jean, this high school teacher. Actually, she looks more like a stripper than a high school teacher. And actually, at one point she was a stripper, but that's another story, and a long one. But we hang out by the pool, you know, we get up at noon when she doesn't have to work, we go down to Mexico sometimes. Our tastes run in the same direction, which is, I think lately, better than love. Or maybe it's the same thing as love. I don't know.

It's just that sometimes, looking back, I think that kid I was knew something then that I don't now. I think I lost something along the way.

And I don't even know what it was. I just remember there was something there, something besides getting the money and then spending the money. I remember the last time I saw Jo, for instance. It was on the morning after my score at Teddy's and I was hot, hot, hot to get to the airport. Vegas couldn't wait for me. I stopped off outside the law school in the rain and waited for her, Petrovsky's ten thousand in an envelope in one pocket, my own thirty thousand in a wad, and when I saw her I knew I had made some kind of mistake. I couldn't even find out where the mistake was. I just knew I'd made one.

I asked her to give Petrovsky the money and she gave me that look, that asshole look, but she didn't ask.

And it was already too late.

But I knew—I knew—that if I only asked her, that if I fell on my knees on the sidewalk and asked her, that she would give me a chance. And I knew that I was right about this, and that I was the right man for her, and the rest was just details. But I was drunk on victory, thirsty for more.

So I kissed her once, there in the rain, and I got in a cab for the airport. And I can see now: this was Teddy's mistake, too, playing to the crowd, playing to the invisible eye that you think is watching. I know now, it isn't watching. But I didn't then. I got in the cab and I left her there on the sidewalk and that was how I got from my life then to my life now. That was the first step.

And all the time we were driving away, I knew that I should go back to her. I was making a mistake and I knew I was making a mistake and that did not stop me. Petrovsky would know. Petrovsky would tell me, too, except that he wouldn't be in his office for another couple of hours and I was in much too big of a hurry to wait around. And I still don't know what I was missing. It keeps me awake sometimes, trying to figure out what it was. It wasn't Jo, not necessarily, though it wasn't necessarily *not* Jo, either. And I don't miss the foolishness. It was something else, though, something I still haven't got. I turn it over and over in my head, lying there at night.

Just something. Something besides winning and losing.

And it's still gone.

I don't know, you know. I think sometimes about my friend Richie Cohen, the one who got beat up so bad they had to take out his spleen. And afterward he was just fine. None of the doctors ever quite told him what a spleen was or why he needed one, when he got along so well without one. I mean, he was just fine. Fine. That's what he said anyway. That's what he told people: I'm just fine. But you knew it couldn't be true.